Yahrah St. John

OHB

"The lighting is all wrong," Avery Roberts commented to a staff member at the Henri Lawrence gallery in Soho, New York. Located on Houston and Broadway, HLG was an eclectic mix of contemporary art.

"How about here?" he tried another position on the wall and glanced in Avery's direction. Everyone knew Avery to be demanding, but he'd never thought so until now. Slender and strikingly beautiful with café-au lait colored skin and light brown eyes and dressed in a fitted grey pants suit and pink silk blouse with a V-neck that revealed a hint of cleavage, she was every man's wet dream. So how could a woman that beautiful be such an ice princess?

Avery smoothed her shoulder-length ponytail and prim bangs with one hand and sighed wearily. "No, no, no," she shook her head. "Move it over there." She ordered, indicating a corner spot in her section of the gallery. It had just the right amount of natural light overhead to reflect her new artist's work.

A buyer at the gallery for several years after attending NYU, Avery knew art. She was well-versed in contemporary, renaissance, baroque and neoclassical art. Ever since she was a child, she'd had a fascination with the craft. Thanks in part to her mother an avid art collector.

"How's it look now?" he asked.

Avery nodded her acceptance. "That's perfect," she replied, walking up to the painting and adjusting it slightly. She was admiring the piece when her boss, the director of the gallery, Hunter Garrett approached.

"I thought it was fine where it was," Hunter commented from her side.

"No," Avery disagreed. "I think the lighting is better here."

"If you say so."

Why did Hunter always have to be so critical? He always had something negative to say about whatever she did because he thought his skills superior to hers. That's why she didn't care an ounce for Hunter Garrett. Sure, he was tall – he was several inches over her five-feet eight, mildly attractive with dark hair and blue eyes, reasonably intelligent and well dressed. Avery just didn't care for his smug attitude or air of bravado.

She'd dated plenty of men just like Hunter having

been raised on Park Avenue because of her father Clayton Roberts, Vice President of Chase Manhattan and her mother Veronica Roberts, queen bee of the socialite arena with whom she'd gone to endless social affairs. Arrogant and conceited, men like Hunter thought the sun rose and set on them.

"Perhaps you should take a break and join me for lunch," Hunter suggested.

"No thanks," Avery politely refused. *Why would he ask her to lunch when he knew she had tons of work to do before the showing tonight?*

"That's too bad," Hunter replied. "I know a great little place in Chinatown that makes the best sushi."

"I don't eat raw fish," Avery lied, walking away from Hunter and heading towards the stairs that housed their small suite of offices. She loved sushi, but she would never admit it to Hunter. "I like mine cooked thank you very much."

"Have it your way," Hunter replied, from the bottom of the stairs.

"I will thank you," Avery feigned a polite smile and rushed up the stairs to her windowless, ten-by-ten office. Once she was safely ensconced within its confines, she fell against the door and breathed a sigh of relief. Somehow she had to get the monkey that was her boss off her back, but how?

"I'M EXCITED to have you back on this side of the Atlantic," talent agent Jason Morgan told his most prized client, photographer Quentin Davis later that morning at his office on Madison Avenue. "Your work has been on point. And if I do say so myself, it's been some of the best of your career."

"Thank you," Quentin appreciated the compliment, but he was dead tired. He had just flown in on the red-eye from London and barely had time to drop off his bags and shower at his loft in Soho before coming to Jason's office. He'd changed out of his favorite pair of Sean John jeans, sketchers and a fitted tee into a more appropriate cashmere cable-knit pullover sweater and trousers for his business meeting.

The problem was he'd stayed a day too long in London for a farewell party thrown by some of his fellow free-lancing buddies and now he was jet-lagged and he had no one to blame but himself.

"The pictures you took over in Ukraine are commanding a high price point. Your stay abroad has been very lucrative," Jason commented on Quentin's recent projects.

Quentin smiled. He couldn't complain. He now had a loft in New York and flats in London, Paris and Rome. Gone were the days of trying to rub two nickels together, his freelancing photography had turned him into a wealthy man and made him one of the most sought-after photographers in the business.

"That's why we have to stay on top of it," Jason continued. "We have to strike while the iron's hot. Warner Books has approached me about publishing some of your work and Entrepreneur would like you to do a photo spread on one of the most powerful men in New York. This could be very lucrative for you."

"Sounds great, Jason." Quentin plopped down in the ergonomic leather chair and ran his hands over his bald head. "But I'm exhausted. Five years overseas working non-stop has taken its toll on me. I need a vacation."

Quentin rubbed the sleep from his eyes and he looked around Jason's office. It was way too early for him to be up. He'd forgotten what it was like to be up before noon. He hated the un-spontaneity of a nine-to-five job. He liked his carefree lifestyle where work was work, but you took time to enjoy life. Americans were too caught up in the rat race. Europeans were so much more laid back, thought Quentin.

And the women . . . well he didn't trust the lot of them. Sure, they were good in the physical pleasure, but as he'd grown more successful in his career as a photojournalist, so had the expectations of the women he'd dated. After several months, many of them wanted a ring on their finger and the security life as his wife would provide. But he wasn't falling for it. He would not be duped by the gold-diggers of the world. His success was his own and one that was hard to come after growing up in an orphanage with his best friends: Malik Williams, Dante Moore and Sage Anderson.

"How long are we talking about?"

Quentin shrugged. "A couple of weeks should do."

Jason sighed. "Oh thank God. I thought you were about take a leave of absence, which I would have advised against. You're a hot commodity right now and one of my best clients."

"I'm sure," Quentin smiled. Jason had made a fortune off Quentin's hard work. "All I want to do for the next couple of weeks is relax."

"All right then. Take a few weeks and call me when you're ready to get back to work."

"Sure thing," Quentin said, rising from his seat. "I'll call you soon." Once he was outside, Quentin took a deep breath of the spring air. He was on his way to run some errands when his cell-phone vibrated in his pants pocket.

"Hello?" Quentin answered.

"Welcome home, Q!" His friend Sage Anderson shouted from the other end. "It's been way too long."

Quentin grinned from ear-to-ear. Sage was his only female friend and he loved her to pieces. She was like his little sister. Perhaps being back in New York wouldn't be so bad after all. "Sage, it's so good to hear your voice, baby girl."

"You too," Sage replied. "How long has it been?"

"Too long."

"Well, I'm dying to see you?" Sage said excitedly as she flipped the page on a new labor case she would take over as lead attorney. "When can we meet?"

"I'm a free agent for a few weeks, so what time would be good for you?"

"How about after work?" Sage suggested. "You know Dante has opened up a tapas bar. We can all meet there."

Quentin rubbed his goatee. "Yes, I had heard and that sounds fantastic!" *And it was about time,* Quentin thought. Dante had been a sous-chef for years. He'd cooked for all of them since they'd left the group home at eighteen and Sage at seventeen to live on their own. Tired of the system, they'd been eager to live life on their own terms.

"Say six o'clock?"

"See you there."

AVERY WAS SO busy checking every last-minute detail from the lighting to music to the caterers that she didn't notice her best friend Jenna Chambers was one the first guests to arrive.

"Avery," Jenna came toward her and gave her a quick hug. "Thanks for the invite."

"No need to thank me. You're doing me a favor. I need all the support I can get," Avery replied. She was extremely nervous about Gabriel's first showing. Although Hunter had given her free reign because she'd handpicked their new artist Gabriel Thomas, she was sure he was hoping tonight was a bust, which would prove to him that she still had a long way to go when it came to picking new talent.

"And you have it," Jenna said. "Don't sweat. Tonight is going to be just fine. You've been to a million of these things before. And look at you." Jenna grabbed Avery by the hand and twirled her around. "You look classy as always."

Avery was wearing a tapered black Chanel pantsuit and peep-toe Jimmy Choo pumps. "Though I would prefer you look hot, but that's okay. One of these days, I am going to get my hands on you and take you down to the Dominic Sabatani Salon for a complete makeover from head to toe." She disliked Avery's perfectly cut bangs and long hair which was in a perfectly coiffed bun.

Unlike Jenna, who was a talent scout for the Wilhelmina Agency where appearance was crucial, Avery didn't need to look sexy. "I need to look competent and knowledgeable so that patrons will come to me for advice, not snag a man."

"That may be true, but you could stand to loosen up a bit, Avery. Sometimes you're too uptight."

"I am not," Avery retorted. "I just need the show to be a success."

"Is the gallery not doing well?" Jenna inquired, grabbing a crab wonton off the platter the waiter was serving and adding it to the two she was already holding in her napkin. "Hmmm, these hors d'oeuvres are to die for."

"What was that?" Avery hadn't been paying attention. She was watching several buyers peruse Gabriel's oil paintings.

"I asked if the gallery was in trouble."

"Oh no," Avery turned her head and focused back to the conversation at hand. "We're doing fine. There are enough wealthy people in New York to keep us afloat, but you can never be too careful."

"Your mother being one of them," Jenna chuckled.

Avery agreed. "Yes only the very best for my mother." Veronica Roberts was the crème de la crème of New York elite and prided herself on supporting local arts. Her contemporary art collection was one of the finest.

Avery supposed that's why she'd chosen art history as a major at NYU. At a young age she'd been exposed to the finer things in life. From their Park Avenue apartment to the best schools, ballet and piano lessons, Avery was never in doubt that she must excel and be the best at everything she did.

She'd incurred her mother's wrath when she'd adamantly refused her mother's help in obtaining a position at an art gallery. With her mother's connections, Avery could have easily procured a job at a well-known gallery instead of a smaller one like HLG, but Avery was determined to stand on her own two feet without any help from mama bear. And tonight, she would show her mother and Hunter that she was more than just a pretty face.

"QUENTIN, it is so good to have you home." Sage squeezed her best friend's shoulders later that evening when they met up after work at Dante's new tapas bar in Greenwich Village, appropriately named *Dante's*.

Quentin returned the hug with equal fervor. He'd missed Sage. She had come a long way from being a frail eight-year-old girl in need of protection. Now she was a beautiful, poised young woman with smooth brown skin and a lovely shape to boot. The ultra-chic, ultra-short pixie cut suited her round face. And although she was only five-foot-three, she could be a tigress and extremely protective of the people she loved and he was proud to be considered one of them.

Of course, he'd missed his boys too. Five years overseas was a long time to be away from his friends when they were the only family he'd ever known.

"Why did you stay away so long?" Sage punched him in the shoulder. "You know New York is where you belong. Isn't that right boys?" Sage glanced at their long-time friends Malik Williams and Dante Moore.

Malik and Dante couldn't be any more different, thought Sage. Malik was brown skin, brooding, wore dreads and preferred Afrocentric dashiki, faded jeans and Birkenstock sandals, while her more level-headed friend Dante was caramel-colored, clean-cut and dressed in trousers, matching vest and a button down shirt.

"Sage is right. We missed you," Dante said, patting Quentin on the back. "It's been too long, Q."

"Well what can I say?" Quentin shrugged. "I got used to my bohemian way of life abroad. Where time stands still and there's no time limits. No restrictions." Whenever he wanted, he would take long breaks from the hard realities of Ukraine and Israel and spend some time in one of his flats.

"New York wasn't the same without you, Q," Sage said.

"You mean you weren't the same without him," Malik chuckled.

Sage turned and glared at Malik. "Same thing. So? How was your first day back in the real world?"

"It was fine. Actually, it was great because I told my agent I was taking a much-needed vacation." Quentin pulled up a barstool next to Malik.

"I don't believe it," Malik said. "Mr. Workaholic is actually going to take a vacation?"

"How long?" Dante piped in.

"A few weeks."

"Wow, I'm shocked," Malik said.

Quentin shrugged. "It was time. Plus, I missed you guys."

"Well, I couldn't be happier," Sage beamed. "Now we can get reacquainted."

"Let's drink to your return," Dante suggested and went behind the bar. He pulled out several shot glasses and some Cuervo Tequila, their former drink of choice, and set them on the bar. He poured generous shots and pushed them toward the trio.

"To the return of Camelot," Malik said, holding up his shot glass.

"To the return of Camelot!" They all cheered, clicked

shot glasses and swished the burning liquid down their throats.

Afterward, Quentin turned his shot glass over and said, "What do you say we get out of here? While I was out at a coffeeshop earlier I heard about a new artist's showing tonight at a gallery in Soho and they always have free food."

"You don't want to eat here?" Dante asked, clutching his heart. "I think I'm offended."

"Of course not, Dante," Quentin replied, leaned over the bar and patted his shoulder. "But I've been out of the art scene for way too long and need to get my feet wet. There will be plenty of nights spent here, my friend."

"I'm on board," Sage replied. Even though Quentin said he was sticking around, Sage figured she had better spend as much time with him as possible before he bolted out of town for greener pastures.

"Well, I can't," Dante replied. "I have to stay here and keep an eye on my investment." His tapas bar had only been open for less than a year, which was make or break for a new business and Dante couldn't afford to fail. He'd put all his savings from years spent as a sous-chef into the restaurant and thus far it was barely making a profit. Several patrons were inside and he had to make sure they had the best tapas experience ever, so they would come back *and* tell their friends.

"I understand completely," Quentin replied. "How about you Malik?"

"Sure, I'll come. Anytime I don't have to cook is always

a good thing." Malik slipped off the stool. "Dante, pass me my bag." He accepted the bag and threw it over his shoulder.

They left several minutes later and took the Blue line to the Henri Lawrence Gallery in Soho. They were there within fifteen minutes. Quentin, Sage and Malik scammed their way past the hostess checking invitations downstairs and climbed up to the main room on the second floor. The gallery was not as trendy as the galleries in London, but did have a red carpet at the front door. Coat check and waiters serving haute appetizers along with several B-list celebrities certainly gave it the appearance of being posh, thought Quentin.

Usually on par, Quentin, however, found himself a tad under dressed amongst this crowd of suit and ties and cocktail frocks.

"Quentin, I think we missed the mark on this one," Malik replied. His dashiki and Birkenstocks certainly did not fit in. At least Quentin fared better in his pull-over sweater and trousers.

Sage sighed. "We're here now. You're just going to have to work it." Sage strutted past several onlookers in her Michael Kors wrap dress and knee-high leather boots to grab three flutes of champagne from the waiter. She returned and handed them each a flute. "See how easy that was."

"Yes, that was easy for you," Malik replied. "Because look at you." He glanced sideways at her. "You look like you just stepped off the pages of a fashion magazine."

Quentin laughed. He admired Sage's confidence and followed her lead by following the waiter across the room and taking several hors d'oeuvres off the platter. He popped a few into his mouth.

"Crashing the party, are we?" Avery asked, leaning against a column nearby. She had seen him and his crew of misfits arrive and by the looks of them, it was clear they weren't on her invitation list.

If she had invited him, she was sure she'd remember. He was tall, dark and handsome. Bald with a sexy goatee and wearing a diamond stud in his ear, he was edgy and certainly not her type, but for some reason she couldn't turn away. The cable pullover sweater he wore did nothing to hide his athletic physique and broad shoulders. In fact, it emphasized that a rock-hard body lay underneath. Avery felt her body heat rising and nervously moistened her dry lips.

Hearing the melodic sound of a feminine voice, Quentin turned around. He wasn't surprised to discover it belonged to a tall, slender beauty with brilliant green eyes. Unfortunately, she was wearing a pantsuit that hid all her God-given assets. *Why did women have to dress up like men?*

"Is it that obvious?" Quentin inquired, placing a hand on the column alongside her face.

Avery stared at his hand. She didn't like the feeling of being closed in by this man, or feeling his warm breath against her face or the smell of his masculine cologne wafting through her nose, so instead she eyed him up and down. "What do you think?" she replied.

Quentin couldn't recall a woman who'd looked at him with such total disdain and it was an instant turn-off. Upon closer inspection, he was able to survey her angular face and scrutinize her slim figure. Sure, she was classically beautiful if he cared for skin the color of café-au-lait and long hair held in an unflattering bun with bangs, but she also had a narrow waist and petite breasts, which Quentin didn't care for. He preferred his women curvier and with a lot more meat on their bones. Or maybe he was just peeved by the sarcastic tone in her voice?

"Perhaps you and your friends," she pointed to Sage and Malik, "should think twice about your attire the next time you crash a party as I'm sure this is not your first." She pushed up from the column, ducked underneath his arm and turned to face him.

"Ouch." Quentin feigned being hurt and touched his chest. "Do you always draw blood at first bite?"

"Only when provoked," Avery returned cattily, folding her arms across her chest even though she wanted to smile at his clever come-back.

"I'm really not as bad as I appear," Quentin tried a different approach by explaining himself, which he never did. He didn't know why he was now; perhaps it was the way she scoffed at him? "I've been in London for a while and flew in this morning on the red-eye. I admit I'm a little tired."

"And in need of a free meal, I presume?" Avery arched an eyebrow.

"So, I take it you think I'm some bum off the street, a freeloader?"

"Aren't you?" she asked, circling around him. And as she did, she received a tantalizing view of his tight rear-end. "Here for the free food and drink, that is? I doubt you even know the first thing about art."

"Listen, lady," Quentin began. He didn't appreciate being insulted by a virtual stranger who knew nothing about the hardships he'd endured. He hadn't grown up with a silver spoon in his mouth. "You don't know the first thing about me."

Avery narrowed her eyes. "And I don't care to." She didn't need to. Con artists like him were a dime a dozen in New York. They were always trying to rip good people out of their money. Avery lumped the stranger in the same category as the beggars on the street.

"Is everything all right over here?" Jenna had returned carrying several cheese puffs and mini-quiches. She glanced back and forth at Avery and batted her eyelashes at the tall, dark, handsome man.

"Everything's just fine," Quentin answered, sipping on his champagne. "It appears your friend thinks I'm a lazy freeloader here only for the free food and drink."

Jenna chuckled. "Hey, so am I." She playfully touched his shoulder with her fingertips. "You should try the mini-beef Wellingtons. They are to die for."

"Thanks for the 411." Quentin glared at Avery one final time and walked away.

Avery breathed a sigh of relief once he'd walked way. He'd upset her equilibrium when she needed to be calm and cool headed for the evening.

"What was that all about?" Jenna inquired. "I sensed some sexual tension in the air."

"There was nothing sexual between me and that man," Avery replied, watching Quentin underneath hooded eyes.

"If you say so," Jenna replied. "But if you ask me, there should have been. You did happen to notice how fine he was."

"I wasn't looking." Avery lied again. She hadn't missed that twinkle in his eyes when he spoke or those luscious lips or the way her stomach had curled at the silken sound of his sexy baritone voice.

'Hmmph' was all Jenna could mutter. She didn't buy for one minute that Avery wasn't the least bit attracted.

From across the room, Quentin took the other woman's advice and munched on some mini-beef Wellingtons. She was much more his type. Beautiful face, large bosom, curvy bottom and completely feminine, just the way he liked his women.

"So, my boss tells me that I have to find the next labor case or my head's on the chopping block," Sage was venting when Quentin rejoined her conversation with Malik. "Can you believe that?"

"Then I suggest you chop, chop," Malik replied.

As Sage discussed her no-win situation, Quentin stood

beside them fuming at the audacity of that ice queen. She hadn't tried to hide her obvious contempt for him and his friends crashing her party.

"What do you think, Q?" Sage inquired.

"What was that?" Quentin asked, distractedly.

"I was telling Malik that my job was in jeopardy."

"At least you have one," Malik interrupted.

"What do you mean?" Quentin asked, "I thought you were working at the community center."

"I am but the King corporation is buying up property on my block all in an effort to build some new entertainment complex and a slew of condos in the neighborhood. If he wins, I'll be out of a job."

"Didn't he buy up another low-income neighborhood a couple of years ago?" Sage inquired. She remembered reading something in the New York Times.

"Yes," Malik answered, "which is why I need your help, Quentin." Malik poked Quentin to get his attention since he was staring across the room again at some woman.

"What do you need?"

"Oh, I don't know. You're the photographer. I thought you could come by the center, take a few photos. You know, showcase what a benefit the center is to the community."

"And if these photos were to end up on the front page of a newspaper or some high-profile magazine then all the better right?" Quentin asked. Malik wasn't slick. He probably figured with his connections a high-profile story might squash the deal.

Malik shrugged matter-of-factly.

"Of course, I'll help," Quentin patted Malik's back. "After everything that center did for us, how could I not? If it weren't for Mr. Webster putting a camera in my hand and showing me, I would not be where I am today. How is the old man anyway?"

"Thanks." Malik bumped his shoulder against Quentin's. "Mr. Webster's getting old and he wants to pass the torch to me, but there may not be a legacy for me to continue."

"I understand," Quentin nodded. "Consider it done. Now, if you'll excuse me." He had some pressing business to attend to.

AVERY NOTICED the stranger had joined Nora Stark, a prominent art buyer. She was sure he couldn't hold his own in a conversation with such a heavyweight and was on her way towards him when Hunter stopped her.

"Avery, how are we doing?" Hunter inquired.

"We've sold five paintings thus far?"

"That's it?" Hunter asked. "Perhaps you ought to be circulating instead of talking to your girlfriend and that party crasher."

So he too had noticed they had party crashers.

"I could throw them out," Avery suggested. "I thought you might not want any negative press tonight, but if I was wrong please let me know?"

Hunter rolled his eyes. "No, no. I agree with you.

Better we allow them a little free food than make a public display."

"Excellent idea," Avery said, "if you'll excuse me." She stalked towards Nora Stark and the stranger whom she was determined to bring down a peg or two.

"Nora," she kissed either cheek of the older Caucasian woman's cheek holding center stage. "How lovely to see you." She noticed the stranger's eyes narrow when she approached.

Nora pulled back and admired Avery's ensemble. "Avery, darling, you're looking splendid as always. How is your mother, dear?"

"Oh just fine. I'm sure she's eager to get started on that charity auction the two of you are heading." *Take that, mystery man!*

"Quentin, have you met Avery?" Nora asked.

Quentin smiled ruefully. "No, I don't believe I've had the pleasure."

"Allow me to introduce you," Nora said, facing the duo. "Avery Roberts, meet Quentin Davis. I'm sure you've heard of Quentin. He's a world-renowned photographer."

If she could have snapped her fingers and made herself disappear, Avery would have. Quentin Davis. *The Quentin Davis.* She loved his work. His pictures on the wars in Ukraine and Israel were moving. Avery was so embarrassed. How could she have been so far off the mark? She'd totally misjudged him.

When Quentin extended his hand, Avery reluctantly accepted. His fingers were cool and smooth as they grazed hers and Avery's skin felt electrified. What was it about this man that caused the hairs on the back of her arm to stand up at attention?

When Quentin locked eyes with the green-eyed ice princess, she was the first to look away. Was that nervousness he saw in her eyes? Surely, he couldn't make her uneasy. He doubted that was even possible.

"I think the two of you should talk while I go peruse my next purchase," Nora said over her shoulder as she departed. "I think you have a lot in common."

"Little does she know," Quentin muttered underneath his breath.

"What was that?"

"Oh nothing," Quentin chuckled to himself.

"So, you . . . you're photographer," Avery stuttered. Did she look as dumb as she sounded? "Why didn't you just tell me who you were?"

"Because you were determined to think I was a bum who couldn't afford his next meal. I was leaving you in a blissful ignorance."

"Did you just call me ignorant?" Avery inquired. *Perhaps, you were,* an inner voice said back. Even so, embarrassment quickly turned to annoyance.

"If the shoe fits," Quentin shrugged.

"You, you, arrogant, son-of-a. . ."

"Now, now," Quentin leaned down so only Avery could hear him. "I'm sure a lady of your social standing wasn't about to use foul language, were you?"

"You know nothing about my social standing," Avery

huffed, taking a step back from Quentin. *Why did the softness of his voice whispering in her ear feel like a lover's tender stroke against her skin?*

"Oh please," Quentin replied. "Don't act like that whole kiss-kiss with Mrs. Stark wasn't all about putting me in my place. I may not have grown up wealthy, but I didn't just fall off the turnip truck either." She was condescending, judgmental and wound as tight as a knot. Avery's face burned with fury. She couldn't stand that he saw right through her. Or that his nearness was playing havoc with her body. "I'm sorry if I offended you, but you have to admit you did give me a reason to judge you."

"To be a snob?" Quentin queried. "For some reason, I think that comes naturally."

"Well, since I disgust you so much, why don't you stay out of my way for the duration of the evening?"

"Gladly," Quentin stormed away, leaving an upset Avery staring at his retreating form. She wanted to yell at him to get back here so she could be the one to walk away, but he was already back with his friends.

"Who ruffled your feathers?" Sage asked, when Quentin returned with a scowl on his face. Malik had abandoned her in favor of hitting on a fellow dreaded woman. "I'll have a Cosmo," Sage said to the bartender. "That ice princess over there." Quentin nodded toward Avery who was giving him the evil eye.

"You mean the one wearing the Chanel suit and wearing a fabulous pair of Jimmy Choo shoes?" Sage accepted the drink from the bartender and took a generous sip.

"Yes, the very one."

"Sounds to me like she voiced me an opinion which many of the airheads you typically date don't have," Sage commented. "Don't take offense, Q; I just call it as I see it."

"I'm not offended. Because you're right. I like my women docile and pliant," Quentin replied. He didn't want some opinionated, repressed, upper crust broad, who wouldn't know passion if it bit her in the butt. He intended to stay as far out of her way as humanely possible.

TWO

very rang the doorbell of her parents' four-bedroom
townhome on Park Avenue the following Saturday
because she'd left her keys at home. Their housekeeper
Louisa answered.

"Louisa!" Avery exclaimed.

Louisa had been the Roberts family housekeeper for
over thirty years. She could have long since retired, but
Avery suspected she stayed more for the company than the
paycheck.

"Avery, how's my favorite girl?" Louisa enveloped her
in a deliciously big hug.

"Oh I'm just fine. Where's Mom?"

"She's in the kitchen," Louisa replied, taking her hand.
"C'mon on in and have a cup of tea and some of my homemade oatmeal-raisin cookies. They are hot out of the oven."

"Oh, that sounds delicious," Avery replied, "but I'll

only have one." Although she could eat what she wanted and never gain a pound, Avery tried to eat right.

She found her mother seated in the eat-in kitchen drinking a cup of Earl Grey tea. Casually dressed in Ralph Lauren capris and a tank top with her hair in a chignon, her mother looked like she was off for a day in the Hamptons as opposed to an afternoon of spring cleaning. Her mother was determined to rid her attic of clutter. Unwanted art would go to her favorite museum and several local galleries.

"Mom." Avery leaned down and gave her mother a gentle squeeze and took the seat opposite her next to a place seating. Her mother looked beautiful as always even without makeup. The only way you could tell her age was by the few fine lines around her eyes.

"Have a cup of tea," her mother ordered.

Avery did as she suggested and on cue, Louisa appeared with a teakettle and packet of English Breakfast tea, Avery's favorite. Avery let it steep for several minutes before adding milk and sugar. "Where's Dad?"

"Oh, he's playing racquetball at the club with one of his buddies," her mother replied, "and it's for the best anyway, because he'd be trying to keep junk instead of throwing it out."

Her mother was right. Her father was something of a pack rat. "I spoke with Nora and she told me you did quite well at your showing."

Did her mother have spies? "Yes, we sold eight paintings of Gabriel's work," Avery replied. "I'm really pleased with the outcome because he was my find, you know."

"That's wonderful, dear," her mother said. Even though Avery knew what her mother wasn't saying. And that was, had she invited her, she would have done a lot better. Veronica would have been sure to invite all her friends and Gabriel's show would have sold out. "And to show my support, I purchased two as well."

"Mom, you didn't have to do that." Avery was annoyed that her mother had to meddle. She just couldn't stay out of her affairs.

"What's the harm? I am your mother, after all, and I only want what's best for you."

"Yes, but you know I wanted to do this on my own."

"You don't have to be *alone*. I have connections. This could all have run much smoother if you'd just let me help. Why must you be so stubborn, Avery?" her mother said exasperatedly. "You shouldn't even have to work. You're too ambitious. If you just found yourself a nice husband and settled down, life would be much easier."

"I don't want to *settle down* and I most definitely don't need you questioning my judgment, mother. I get enough of that at work," Avery replied.

"And who's doing that?"

"Hunter Garrett."

"Oh," her mother chuckled. "I've dealt with him before. He's a pussycat. Don't worry about him."

"There you go again, dismissing my feelings as if they

don't count. I wonder why I even bother," Avery said, rising from the table and grabbing her purse.

"Where are you going?"

"I am going someplace where I can feel appreciated," Avery returned, walking out the kitchen. She was tired of her mother's constant criticism that she was too ambitious and too driven. She was quite capable of looking after herself. Avery didn't need to marry some rich guy and be his showpiece. "Tell Daddy I said hello," Avery said over her shoulder as she left.

"WHY HAVEN'T you returned any of my calls," Jenna said, when Avery finally met up with her on Friday evening for dinner. They were standing in the foyer of a new restaurant waiting for a table.

"I'm sorry," Avery apologized as she hung her head low. "It's been a tough week."

"No kidding." Jenna grabbed Avery by the chin and peered into her face. Avery's eyes were puffy and there were lines around her eyes. "Have you gotten enough sleep? You look haggard, my dear."

"Thanks a lot," Avery said, snatching her head away.

"Is everything okay?" Jenna asked. "I can tell something's wrong. You aren't yourself. What's going on?"

The hostess interrupted them before she could answer and led them to an empty table that had suddenly become available.

Avery wasted no time spilling her guts once they were seated. "Oh, the usual. A fight with my mother."

"That seems to be par for the course for you these days."

"Jenna, sometimes she and I are like oil and water. We just don't mix. You think she'd be proud of me that I'm doing so well at the gallery, but she's always quick to point out my shortcomings. Or my single status. A girl of your age," Avery mocked her mother, "should already be married and settled by now."

"She didn't try and set you up again, did she?"

"No, but she would have tried if I'd given her the opportunity."

"Well, forget about her for tonight and let's have some fun. How about dancing after dinner?"

"That sounds like a fabulous idea." Avery could use the distraction.

After dinner, Avery and Jenna found themselves at Blue Note. Known for its late-night grooves and full house, Avery wasn't sure they'd get in, but one of Jenna's former models just so happened to be the bouncer at the door and squeezed them in. As they walked to the bar, Avery spied someone familiar seated at a table with some friends. As she approached, Avery realized it was none other than Quentin Davis, the photographer she'd made a fool out of herself in front of last week.

"Cover me," Avery said, pushing Jenna in front of her.

"Why?" Jenna asked over her shoulder.

Avery didn't answer until they were safely past his

table and seated in a corner by the bar. "You remember that guy from my showing last week."

"You mean that good looking guy you were rude to?" Jenna asked. "Then yes, I remember him."

"Well, he's over there." Avery motioned with her head toward the front of the room. When Jenna went to turn around, Avery stopped her. "Don't look. You'll draw attention to us. Let's just stay over here and hopefully they'll leave soon."

"You hope."

"Yes, I do," Avery replied. The last thing she needed was another round with Quentin Davis.

ACROSS THE ROOM, Quentin, Sage, Malik and Dante were having a good time laughing and reminiscing about the good ole days.

"Do you remember when Mr. Webster caught us sneaking back in after curfew?" Dante asked.

"Oh yeah, we had just turned sixteen, gotten a fake ID and decided we were grown enough to go out on our own," Malik continued.

"That's until we got jumped by those older guys, had all our money stolen and ended up walking twenty blocks home in the rain," Quentin remembered.

"And then Mr. Webster caught us and put us on dish detail for a month," Dante finished.

"Yeah, those were the days," Malik replied.

Sage's brow furrowed. "Why don't I remember that story? Where was I?"

"That's because you were only fourteen, kiddo, and we had to leave you at home," Quentin teased as he rose to his feet. "And you did nothing but sulk for days that you had been left out of all the excitement."

"I did not," Sage returned. Even though she recalled being somewhat of a brat afterward.

"You did too," Quentin whispered in her ear as he leaned down. Once he made it to the bar, he ordered a bucket of Miller Lite and was glancing around the room when his eyes rested on a female frame at the corner of the bar. It was that ice queen from the gallery who'd treated him like he'd crawled out of the gutter.

Great, thought Quentin. The air in the bar suddenly turned chilly. The bartender slid him a bucket and Quentin slipped him a twenty. "Keep the change."

Quentin slid back into his seat with a frown. "Guess who's here?" he asked.

"Who?" Sage asked, looking around.

"Remember that woman from the gallery?"

"The one in the Chanel suit who was pissed we crashed her showing?"

"The one and only," Quentin replied.

"Why don't you go over and say hello?" Sage suggested. "You know, get off on a better foot?"

"I don't think so," Quentin said, "that woman's as cold as ice."

"Remember when we used to make bets with each

other to go out with someone and see how long we'd last?" Malik asked. "Well, I'll bet you twenty bucks," he pulled out his wallet and slid a twenty Quentin's way, "that you can't melt that ice queen."

"You're joking," Quentin said, pushing the money back towards Malik. "We haven't done that since we were teenagers."

"Who said we ever have to grow up," Dante replied. "Do it. And for added incentive, lets up it to fifty." Dante slid another thirty dollars across the table.

Quentin thought about it for a moment. They thought he couldn't melt the ice around that diva's heart. Sure, it would be difficult, but he was Quentin Davis after all. "All right, you're on." Quentin accepted the bet, tucked the bills in his pocket, grabbed his bottle of beer and stood up ready to face off against the lady dragon.

"Wait!" Sage yelled when Quentin started to walk away. She jumped up from her chair and slid another fifty bucks in his pockets. "Don't leave me out." Sage kissed Quentin on the cheek, smacked him on the butt and said, "Go get her tiger, urgh."

Quentin strutted to the back of the bar and walked up to Avery Roberts, who was sitting at the bar with her back to him. She was with that sexy friend of hers from the showing. Quentin would have preferred if the bet was on her as it would be much more enjoyable, but alas it wasn't. "Uh huh," Quentin coughed. When Avery didn't turn around, he coughed again.

Avery swiveled around in her barstool and was

surprised to find Quentin standing behind her. "What do you want?" Avery asked a little too sharply.

Although Quentin didn't care for her tone, he persevered. He was always up for a challenge. Quentin smiled and said, "Ladies." He nodded over to her friend.

"Hi, how are you?" Jenna smiled back flirtatiously.

"Oh, I'm fine," Quentin replied. "I'm just here with some friends listening to the jazz band. They're great, aren't they?" Quentin asked, placing his beer bottle on the bar.

"Yes," Avery said curtly. "Now, can I help you with something?" She ignored Jenna, who was glaring at her.

Quentin took a deep breath and willed himself to calm down before responding. "Well, I came over to apologize for last week." At Avery's blank stare, he continued, "You know, crashing your showing. My friends and I really shouldn't have come without an invitation and I apologize. I hope we didn't cause you any trouble."

Avery was shocked when Quentin apologized. She hadn't seen that one coming. Now she felt two-feet small because once again, she'd misjudged him. But this time instead of insulting him, she'd be the bigger person. Especially since being angry took too much energy and after arguing with her mother she was fresh out. "No apologizes necessary. No harm. No foul."

"Great," Quentin smiled. And when he did, Avery's heart skipped a beat. Why is it she hadn't noticed what a great smile he had? Could it be because she was too busy judging him? Perhaps he'd been right last week when he'd implied she was judgmental. She would have to work on that. "So, how about I buy you ladies a drink?"

Her initial thought was to say no thank you, but then Avery thought better of it. "Thank you, I'd like that," she said instead.

"Bartender, I'll have two . . . ," he glanced over at their empty glasses.

"Espresso martinis," Avery offered.

"Two espresso martinis, please," Quentin said. When the barkeep returned with two glasses, Quentin handed each of the women one and raised his bottle. "To new beginnings."

"To new beginnings." Avery and Jenna chimed in and clinked glasses before sipping their martinis. From her perched view atop the barstool, Avery was nearly face to face with Quentin and what a face it was. Avery allowed herself to enjoy the view. Smooth sexy chocolate skin, broad nose, full lips and a glistening bald head made Quentin Davis one very attractive man. He was wearing a royal blue silk shirt, tucked into black trousers along with two pieces of jewelry, the diamond stud she'd seen before in his ear and a St. Christopher cross dangled from his neck.

The band struck up a slow ballad and couples began filling up the small dance floor. Quentin realized that a slow dance was a prime opportunity to make his move and put all the Davis charm on Ms. Roberts.

"Would you like to dance?" Quentin asked, chugged the rest of his beer and placed the empty bottle on the bar.

Avery shook her head. "I really don't dance. I'm terrible at it. I have absolutely no rhythm."

Quentin chuckled. "You can't be that bad." Quentin took the martini glass out of her hand, placed it on the bar and pulled Avery to her feet.

"No," Avery pulled away. "I'm really that bad. Why don't you take, Jenna?" Avery glanced in her friend's direction, but Jenna shook her head.

"He didn't ask me," Jenna replied. "And I'm finishing my drink anyway."

"There, it's settled," Quentin placed his hand on the small of Avery's back and led her to the dance floor much to her dismay.

"I warn you, I'm very bad," Avery commented.

"Don't worry, I'll lead," Quentin said, encircling her waist with his arm and pulling her toward him. Thanks to the crowded dance floor, they were thigh-to-thigh and cheek-to-cheek. When Avery tried to put some distance between, Quentin pulled her closer until her small pert breasts were resting firmly against chest. Slowly and deliberately, Quentin moved her slender body with his to the rhythm of the music.

Being so close to Avery allowed Quentin an opportunity to inspect the ice queen and see what he'd really gotten himself into with this bet. His first thought was that she smelled fantastic. Soft, light and airy, she smelled fresh and ripe for the picking. His second thought was that she was much prettier than he'd originally thought, especially if she did a little bit more with her hair rather than having it pinned up all time. Quentin wished he could take out every pin and run his fingers through her long hair and make it unruly. Avery Roberts needed to be cut loose from her restraints.

As Quentin glided her across the dance floor, with one big strong hand clasped firmly in hers, Avery wasn't surprised to find that he was a skillful dancer. He looked like the sort to know how to move a woman's body. She tried not to peer into his arresting dark eyes for fear she'd get lost in them and step on his feet. Quentin kept her on the floor through several slow tunes and didn't release his hold on her until the tempo changed.

"See, you're not as bad as you think," Quentin whispered in her ear once the dance was over.

"That's because you were guiding me," Avery said. "Anyway, thanks for the dance."

"You're welcome," Quentin replied, "maybe we can do it again sometime."

"Maybe," Avery said.

Quentin joined her back at the bar but not before glancing at his friends who were giving him an enthusiastic thumbs-up. Quentin smiled. Avery may not know him, but his friends knew him well enough to know and she would be putty in his hands in no time. Quentin wasn't arrogant about his prowess. He just knew he had a way with women and he had an oversized black book to prove it with names from across the Atlantic.

"Aren't you going to rejoin your friends?" Avery inquired. "You don't have to stay and keep us company."

"Perhaps I find your company more appealing," Quentin said silkily.

"I, uh . . ." Avery couldn't think of a proper come-back. Why did he have to say things that? Was he trying to throw her off-kilter?

"Well, I'm exhausted." Jenna faked a yawn and stretched her arms. "I think I'm going to head out." Jenna stood up, reached for her clutch purse and plopped her credit card on the bar. "After everything you've been through this week, drinks are on me tonight."

"Jenna," Avery turned and pleaded with her eyes for her best friend to stay, but Jenna ignored her and settled the bill with the bartender. When she was done, she leaned over and whispered in her ear. "Relax and enjoy." She gave one final wave before exiting.

"What did Jenna mean after everything you've been through?" Quentin inquired.

"It's been a tough week."

"I'm sorry to hear that," Quentin said, taking the stool vacated by Jenna. "Perhaps I can remedy that."

"Not so fast, Mr. Quentin Davis." Avery placed a hand on his chest. And when she did, Avery wished she hadn't. Quentin's chest was broad and rock-hard. "Just because we shared a dance does not mean anything is going to happen here."

"Must you always be so combative?" Quentin asked. "A drink and a few laughs amongst friends might cure your bad mood."

"So we're suddenly bosom buddies now?" Avery queried. "You don't even like me very much."

"I thought we were off to a brand-new start," Quentin replied, "but if I was wrong . . ." He rose to his feet.

When he did, Avery realized she didn't want him to go. "No, no, you weren't wrong. Sit back down."

That's when Quentin knew he had her.

"I'm sorry," Avery apologized and shook her head. "Listen. It's not you. It's me. I'm going through a rough patch right now and although I appreciate the drink. I'm really tired and going to head home."

"Sure I can't tempt you to have another drink?" Quentin asked. He'd seen the anguish in her eyes.

"Not tonight." Avery stood up, turned on her heel and walked out the door, leaving a frustrated Quentin in her wake.

His charm usually worked on most women, but apparently not Avery Roberts. It had only worked as much as she'd allowed it to work out on the dance floor. For a moment he'd gotten to her, but just as quickly the moment passed. He was going to have to work a lot harder to get closer to Avery.

He returned to the table where his friends sat with gigantic smirks on their faces. "What's wrong playa? Did she shut you down?" Malik joked.

"Seems someone has bitten off more than he could chew," Dante chuckled.

"Oh leave him be," Sage said. *Trust my little sis to*

always defend me, thought Quentin. "Forget them." Sage turned to Quentin. "You said she was a cold fish."

Quentin shook his head. "It wasn't that. There was something else."

"An aversion to playas," Malik suggested.

Quentin laughed from deep within his belly. "No, not that either. Something was troubling her. Something so profound, it's rocked her to the core. I could see it in her eyes even though she was putting on a brave front."

"Then you're just in time to help a damsel-in-distress," Dante replied. "It's Quentin to the rescue."

"If I didn't love you so much, I'd have to hurt you." Quentin laughed.

"So, what's next?" Sage asked.

"I don't know." Quentin rubbed his goatee. "I'm going to think about it. Because trust me, the next time I meet Avery Roberts, she will not walk away."

"Those are some big words, my man," Malik said. "Now let's see if you can back them up."

"Oh he can back them up," Sage nodded.

"You better believe I can," Quentin nodded.

THREE

"Daddy, it's so good to hear from you," Avery said when he telephoned her later that week. "What's going on?"

"I was hoping you would make up with your mother," Clayton Roberts said from the other end of the line. "She still wants your help cleaning out the attic."

"Daddy . . ."

"You know how your mother can get," her father said.

"You mean critical and controlling?" Avery asked bitterly.

"No, I mean overprotective. You know she only wants what's best for you."

"She has a funny way of showing it," Avery huffed. If she didn't have anything nice to say she shouldn't say anything at all.

"Have you ever thought you're being overly sensitive?"

Avery paused. Perhaps he had a point. Her mother did

have a way of getting to her and she let her. "All right, I will make amends," Avery replied, "but only for you." She was a Daddy's girl after all. He always seemed to understand her more than her mother. He never criticized, instead he just offered an ear or a suggestion to listen whenever she had a problem. He never tried to control the outcome.

"Good, sweetheart. I'll see you later on Saturday then."

"Bye, Daddy."

QUENTIN DECIDED that since he had all this extra free time, he could finally stop by the old neighborhood in Harlem and visit the community center he, Malik, Dante and Sage had frequented as children. The center had been an oasis for them after having been seen as a bunch of misfits at the orphanage; the troublemaker, the angry boy, the nerd and the sickly girl.

As he walked the streets of Harlem after exiting the Blue train, Quentin was surprised at how much the place had stayed the same. Sure, there were some pockets that even he wouldn't be caught dead on in the middle of the night, but all in all not much had changed. It was sure a far cry from his current digs in Soho. Quentin smiled to himself as he opened the tattered front door of the center. He'd come along way, although the same could not be said for the door.

He gave his name to the receptionist at the front counter and signed his name on the guest list. She wasn't

Vivienne Falconer, the old battle-ax who used to give him, Malik and Dante a hard time, but she looked as if she could check a young brother if needed and scare him into behaving and acting right. She waved him to come on back and that's just what he did.

Malik came rushing out a side office. "Wow, I'm surprised you came."

Quentin tried not to take offense to his best friend's comment. "You did ask me to come by and take some photographs, or did I miss a beat somewhere?"

"No, of course not," Malik replied. "I'm sorry, Quentin. It's been a trying morning. Come on in." He brought him to his small office. As Quentin looked around, it too was in need of a paint job. Quentin determined right then and there to give a generous donation to fix up the community center. If he had the opportunity to do so and the corporation Malik mentioned didn't take over.

"It's all right," Quentin laughed and settled back into a chair across from Malik's desk. "If I didn't love you like a brother, I might be offended. But since I do, I'll let it slide."

"I am really grateful you came, Q," Malik replied. "The King corporation has been targeting several store owners on this block and offering them big checks to sign over their property and now the community center has been approached."

"What are you going to do?"

"I have no intention of selling to the King corporation so that fat cats like Richard King can get richer and richer while the poor in this community are displaced."

"What can I do to help?"

"I need you to use all your connections and put a big spotlight on this, so that the community and beyond is aware of what's happening." Malik stood up as he gave his impassioned speech. "The people in this community are looking to the center to help, to stop this travesty from happening. Many of these store owners have owned their property for years, before the King Corporation had any interest in *re-developing* it."

"I know a lot of big names that would eat a story like this up," Quentin replied. He could see it spread across the New York Times or Post: big corporation versus low-income community. "I'll call up a few contacts. Otherwise, I am at your disposable."

"It's been awhile since you've been back," Malik said. "Why don't you walk around, get a feel for the place and take some of those candid photographs you take that capture a nation. In the meantime, I have some paperwork to finish up here."

"Sure thing." Quentin stood up and threw his camera bag over his shoulder. He didn't need Malik to give him a tour of the community center because it had been his second home in his youth.

The center housed a computer and dance room, basketball court, swimming pool and clinic for free health and dentistry for the community. The neighborhood relied on the free health care the center provided along with the headstart and after-school kids programs. He stopped by each of them to take pictures. He hoped to use his camera as a tool to show the unseen or the forgotten people that this center helped. And he did just that. He got some great shots of the dancers in class with their graceful movements, but his favorite shots were of the toddlers because they'd captured the wide-eyed innocence of youth. As he strolled down the halls, Quentin realized just how much responsibility Malik had on his shoulders.

His final stop was the basketball courts where several male teenagers were shooting hoops. Quentin quietly came in and stood along the sidelines. As he snapped photos, one of the young men looked over at him and then nudged his friends.

"Hey! What you doing with that camera?"

"Just taking a few pictures," Quentin replied, "I hope you don't mind."

"That depends on what you're going to do with them?" His friends chuckled behind him.

"Well. . ." Quentin rubbed his goatee. "They might end up in a news magazine or perhaps on television."

"Why? Are you famous?" the young man inquired. "'Cause I sure don't know you."

"In a way yes, I'm a photojournalist."

"What's that?" another boy asked.

Quentin shook his head. It was a shame that these young men had no idea of what he did for a living because they were not exposed to anything outside their daily lives. Quentin resolved to do all he could to stop this corporate giant from railroading another low-income community.

"I take pictures and sell them to magazines and television stations and they publish them or put them on air."

"Wow, that's kind a cool," the first young man said. "How's the Benjamins on something like that?"

Quentin laughed deep in his belly. "The Benjamins are quite good. But you have to work hard and learn your craft before you really start to get paid," Quentin replied. "Have any of you guys ever taken a photography class here at the center?"

"Photography?" The young man's voice rose. "Naw, man, we 'bout playing ball."

"Life isn't all about basketball and having fun. You should try something new sometime and if you're interested," Quentin continued, "I might be persuaded to come and teach you the basics of photography."

"You would?" The boys sounded shock that he would go out of his way to help them out.

"Yes, I would," Quentin replied honestly, just as Mr. Webster had helped him.

"That sounds like an excellent idea," a masculine voice said from behind him. Quentin turned around and found Malik grinning from ear-to-ear. "You guys need a hobby."

Malik walked toward them. "That's a really generous offer, Quentin." Malik took him aside. "I know how busy you are. If you want to just take the pictures, that's fine with me."

Quentin shook his head and patted Malik's shoulder. "It's no imposition. I could stand to give back a whole lot more."

Malik chuckled. "See," he pointed a knowing finger at Quentin. "You have to work. You can't just relax."

"I've been doing nothing but taking it easy for two weeks now. And if I can open up some young men to the joy of photography, then all the better." He turned back around to the young men. "I'll be back on Monday around 3pm and we can get started. And you," he said to Malik. "I'll see later."

Malik mouthed the words 'thank you' as Quentin headed out the swinging doors.

Quentin was feeling in such a good mood he decided to complete his day by going to the Henri Lawrence Art Gallery where a certain lady just so happened to work. He hadn't forgotten the bet and it was time he paid it due attention.

THE FOLLOWING SATURDAY, Avery arrived as promised and found the attic in complete disarray. Her mother had already gotten started and there were tons of boxes, trunks, exercise equipment, paintings and various sculptures and artifacts from her mother and father's travels over the years and from the looks of it, her parents hadn't gone through anything since she was a child, which made it over thirty years' worth of junk.

"I'm glad to see you could make it," her mother replied, as Avery rolled up her sleeves and donned a scarf to her protect her hair from the dust and spiders.

Avery ignored the dig. "Why don't we tag everything

you do want," Avery suggested, "and we'll throw away what you don't want."

"Good idea," her mother said.

Two hours later, they had made progress and had managed to clear out path to the hallway, but only because Louisa had assisted after finishing her chores.

"I don't know about you guys, but I'm ready for lunch," Louisa spoke up.

"Lunch would be great, Louisa. Can you whip us up some sandwiches?" her mother asked.

"Already done. I pre-made the sandwiches and the soup just needs to be heated up," Louisa replied. "I'll go warm it up now."

When Avery stumbled upon an old chest that had been hidden by some old carpeting, all hell broke loose.

"I wonder what's inside," Avery said. No sooner than the words were out of her mouth, her mother shouted at her. "Don't open that trunk!"

"Why? It's just an old trunk," Avery replied. She was opening the lid, when her mother nearly leapt across the room and shut it. And to make matters worse, she sat on the lid.

"Mother! What's gotten into you?" Avery looked up at her mother. She looked as white as a ghost. She didn't understand what the big deal was. "Is there something in that chest I'm not supposed to see?"

"Of course not," her mother laughed nervously.

"Then why won't you move?" Avery asked.

"If you must know," her mother replied, "there are

some old love letters from your father in that trunk and I'd like them to remain private."

"Is that all?" Avery smiled. "Why didn't you just say so?" Avery rose to her feet.

Her mother didn't have time to answer because Louisa called up to them, Avery's father had returned from his racquetball game and was standing in the doorway. "Hi, pumpkin," he said, glancing at Avery before planting a kiss on her mother's cheek. Her usually well-dressed father was wearing a workout jumpsuit. "Lunch is ready."

"You're just in time for lunch, daddy," Avery replied.

"Well, you know, I don't miss Louisa's homemade soups."

"C'mon, let's go eat." They both headed to the door hand-in-hand, but Avery held back.

Her mother's reaction to that trunk disturbed Avery. The knowledge that her mother could be hiding something caused her to rush over to the trunk. Should she open Pandora's box? Maybe what was inside was best left hidden? Or maybe something critical about her past was inside?

Despite her reservations, Avery opened the lid. Inside were some newborn baby clothes and a swaddling blanket. Was this what she was brought home in? Avery's eyes misted with tears. Why hadn't her mother ever shown her this before? She continued her fact-finding mission by digging through the trunk until she found a portfolio.

Curious, Avery popped open the lock and looked inside. The contents appeared to be important legal documents. Avery quickly scanned them for a clue of what her parents could be hiding when her eyes saw the word "ADOPTION" in big letters across the front page of one of the papers. Avery was in shock as she continued the read the document which stated in plain English, that Mr. and Mrs. Clayton Roberts had adopted an infant baby girl born on September 9, 1973.

"Ohmigod!" Avery fell back in horror and tears streamed down her face. "No, no, this can't be. This can't be." Avery shook her head. *She was adopted!* Her parents weren't really her parents?

A million questions went through Avery's mind as understanding dawned on her. Holding the paper in her hand, Avery realized that this is why her mother didn't want her to open that trunk. She didn't want the truth to come out, which is that they'd been lying to her from the day she was born. What Avery didn't understand was why didn't they tell her? It wasn't like she wasn't old enough to learn the truth. Why had they kept this from her? And if she wasn't Avery Roberts, who was she? Who were her real parents?

Avery wept aloud, rocking back and forth and didn't hear the attic floor creek or see her parents walk in.

"Oh, Avery." Her mother fell to the floor and pulled a distraught Avery in her arms. "Oh baby, I'm so sorry . . ." her mother cried, holding Avery close to her heart.

"So, it's true then?" Avery asked through a haze of tears as she held onto her mother for dear life. "I'm adopted?"

Silence ensued, fracturing whatever thread of hope Avery had that the document wasn't real.

Her mother nodded her head. "Yes, but we never wanted you to find out this way. We wanted to tell you."

"Why didn't you?" Avery choked out. "Why didn't you tell me?"

Her father kneeled down beside her. "I don't know, baby girl. I suppose we were just selfish and wanted you all to ourselves. Ever since the day you were born, you've been the light of our lives."

"My whole life has been a lie."

"That's not true." Her mother shook her head.

Avery flung herself out of her mother's arms. Her father tried to help her from the floor, but Avery refused his help and rose on her own. "How can you say that? Everything has changed. I don't even know who I am."

"You are our daughter, Avery Roberts," her mother's voice stated vehemently. "Nothing has changed."

"That's not true. You lied to me. You should have told me long ago that I was adopted. My God, I've always wondered why people said I looked nothing like the two of you. Why I always felt out of place, like a square peg in a round hole."

When her parents stared at one another without answering, Avery yelled at them. "Where does a black girl with green eyes who looks almost white come from? Where do I come from?"

Avery was upset because her father was doing his stoic routine while her mother hung her head low and remained silent. "Where do I come from? Answer me!" A hot exultant tear trickled down Avery's cheek.

Her father was the first to speak. "What do you want to know?"

"I want to know about my biological mother?" Avery asked, folding her arms across her chest.

"Your birth mother was very young and she wasn't ready to be a parent. We preferred not to know her name," her mother replied.

Avery nodded and wiped a tear from her cheek with the back of her hand. "That explains her reasons for giving me up. What were yours for adopting?"

When her mother finally spoke she stammered. "I'll . . . I'll answer that." She rose to her feet. "Your father and I wanted a newborn. We were evaluated and screened like any another adoptive parents."

"That doesn't answer my question," Avery replied.

"Avery does it really matter?" her father asked. He knew this was a touchy subject with Veronica and he didn't want his wife or his daughter to suffer any more than what was needed.

"Yes, it does," Avery said adamantly.

Her mother walked over to the small window overlooking the tree-lined street and stared listlessly out of it. Silence ensued in which neither of her parents spoke.

When her mother finally turned around, her cheeks were stained with tears. It hurt Avery to see her mother in pain, but she would not be dissuaded. She wanted the whole truth and nothing but. She deserved that much.

"We adopted you because I couldn't have any children," her mother said. "I couldn't give your father a child and despite my shortcomings he stayed with me. He vowed we'd have a family someday and we did. We had you."

"Oh Veronica." her father came toward her mother and pulled her into his arms. She collapsed in his arms, but he didn't let go, he just held on tighter.

"I know this is difficult for you, but imagine what this is like for me," Avery said. "I need answers."

"Honey, now is not the right time," her father said over his shoulder. "Can't you see your mother is upset?"

Turning blindly, Avery grabbed the adoption papers and stumbled down the stairs. She couldn't stand it anymore. Knowing that her loving parents, the people she confided in and trusted the most had betrayed her was beyond unbearable.

Seeing Avery upset, Louisa instinctively called out to her, but Avery shook her head, grabbed her jacket off the coat rack and rushed out the door.

Somehow she managed to hail a cab and once inside she fell against the backseat. Her whole world was falling apart. Avery covered her mouth with her hand and smothered the grief that threatened to spill out should she move her hand. How could this be happening?

A short while later as she rode the elevator up to her apartment on the Upper East Side, the future looked bleak. Her mind was spinning and she had no idea how she was supposed to go on after learning her life was built on a lie. Once she made it inside her apartment, she immediately felt sick to her stomach and barely made it the bathroom before purging the contents in her stomach. Afterwards, she fell down on the floor and let out a gut-wrenching sob.

AVERY'S EMOTIONS raged over the weekend as she reeled from the knowledge that she was adopted. She tried drowning her sorrows on the piano by playing sad music. When that didn't work she did the one thing that usually made her better and that was making pottery. Once she felt the moist lumps of clay in her hand and she sat over the potter's wheel with her foot on the treadle wheel, Avery felt somewhat calm. But then, out of nowhere, she had a bout of hysteria that had her so debilitated she had to leave the wheel. Hours later, she'd accomplished nothing. Somehow she managed to put one foot in front of the other and make it to work on Monday. She masked her inner turmoil to her co-workers and boss even though she was dying inside.

The only thing she was sure of after she'd cried her eyes out was that she had to find her biological mother. Even if she didn't want to have anything to do with her, Avery had to find out where she came from or at least that's what she told herself. But deep down Avery secretly hoped that her biological mother would want to meet her. Avery knew that it would hurt her parents to hear she was launching a search, but this was something she had to. If she didn't, she would always wonder and never be free.

The problem was when she called the New York State

Department of Health for an original copy of her birth certificate, she found out that they had no record of her having been born in New York and even if she were, all adoptive records were sealed. They suggested she register with reunion agencies or petition the court to open her adoption file. All of which could take a considerable amount of time and Avery had to have answers now. What she needed was to find an honest, reliable private investigator to research her past. Luckily, one of her sorors, Julia Peoples, a fellow Alpha Kappa Alpha from NYU, was a criminal attorney. Avery was sure Julia used investigators in her line of work and if she didn't, she might know where to look.

Picking up the phone, Avery nervously dialed Julia's number; thankfully Julia picked up on the second ring. "Julia, how are you darling, it's Avery."

"Avery, long time no hear," Julia said. "How are you?"

"Oh, I'm just fine," Avery replied trying to sound cheery. "How are things at the law firm? Are you still hoping to make partner this year?"

"I sure am. I've been working my fanny off pulling sixty-hour work weeks in the hopes there will be a big payoff."

"I'm sure it will, Julia. You have the drive and the ambition," Avery replied. "Listen, I was hoping you could do me a favor."

"Anything for a soror."

"Well, I am in need of a private investigator with abso-lute discretion and I was hoping you might know of someone?" Given her parents social standing in the community, she didn't want word of this leaking out.

"Is everything all right, Avery? Are you in some kind of trouble?" Julia inquired. "If so, you know I'll help anyway I can."

"No, no," Avery said. "It's nothing like that. It's nothing criminal. I just need some information."

"All right, let me get his number out of my rolodex." Julia paused for several moments before speaking. "His name is Woody Owen. He's my go-to guy. If someone is hiding something, he'll find it. And Woody will treat you with the utmost confidentiality."

"Excellent," Avery said. "He's just what I need."

Ten minutes later, she had an appointment that afternoon to meet with Mr. Owen at his office near the courthouse.

THE REST OF THE AFTERNOON, Avery was wound up as tight as a cat. She was dying to meet Woody, but Hunter was watching her like a hawk and she didn't dare leave for fear she'd take too long. Walk-in traffic was slow that day and Avery was admiring several abstract paintings when Quentin Davis walked in.

What was he doing here? Avery wondered. Her afternoon had already gotten off to a rocky start and she didn't need the distraction. Every time she was around him for longer than a few minutes, he threw her off balance. She didn't need that today, so she hid behind a wall to prevent him from seeing her.

She watched and admired the man from afar. He exuded raw sex appeal. She didn't know if it was his glistening bald head or the way his jeans hung low to his well-shaped posterior. All she knew was that she was attracted to him and that would never do. He was all wrong for her. She preferred the clean-cut suit-and-tie type. So what was it about Quentin Davis that caused her to get all hot and bothered?

Avery didn't take the time to find out. She scurried off to the ladies room to bring down her rapid pulse and to check her appearance. She smoothed her ponytail and bangs, straightened her diamond heart necklace and checked her lipstick. Satisfied that she looked presentable, Avery exited the restroom and walked toward the front of the gallery. She found Quentin leaning over the reception desk speaking with the intern they'd recently hired.

She stopped inches from their little tête-à-tête and waited to be acknowledged. Quentin finally glanced in her direction and when he did, Avery nearly froze in place and her breath caught in her throat as he rewarded her with a disarming smile.

"Avery," Quentin straightened and came towards her. "Just the person I was looking for."

"Oh, why was that?" Avery asked, trying to sound nonchalant.

"Well," Quentin started, but then stopped in front of a

painting. "This is an excellent piece of abstract work, don't you think? I love the artist's use of color and form."

"Yes, I agree. Forbes has an amazing gift for depicting objects in an unconventional way, but I doubt you came all this way to discuss art," Avery replied, glancing sideways at Quentin.

"No, I didn't." Quentin shifted his gaze to Avery. He allowed his eyes to travel from her conventional pumps, black wide-leg pants up to her crisp white shirt and black vest.

She tried hard to keep her eyes on the painting, but the way Quentin was staring at her, Avery found it hard to remain focused.

"I came to ask you to dinner."

"Dinner?"

"Yes, you know it's called a date when two people agree to share a meal at the same table." Quentin laughed as he spoke.

"I know what a date is."

"Perhaps you haven't been on one in a while?" Quentin asked. "Which is why you've forgotten. If so, I'd like to remedy that."

"Just because we agreed to be civil doesn't mean I'd agree to share dinner with you," Avery responded.

"Please don't tell me we're back to square one again. I thought we agreed to be friends and if so, you can look on this as a friendly dinner."

Avery was about to answer when Hunter came toward

them. "Mr. Davis," he said, "it's a pleasure to have you at the gallery."

Quentin glanced at the interloper. He didn't appreciate his conversation with Avery being interrupted. "Thank you. And you are?"

"Hunter Garrett, the director of the gallery." Avery watched Hunter puff out his chest like he was some big dog and extend his hand. She despised Hunter's posturing. He didn't hold a candle to Quentin's naturally broad chest.

"Pleasure to meet you, Hunter," Quentin replied, shaking his hand. Then a mischievous thought popped into his head. He could use this peon to help him on his mission. "I was just asking Ms. Roberts to dinner so that we could discuss the possibility of exhibiting some of my work."

"Would you really be interested in an exhibiting in a gallery as small as ours?" Hunter asked.

Avery gave Quentin the evil eye. She knew exactly what he was up to. He was using her job as a way to get her to go out with him. She could strangle him!

"I could be persuaded over dinner if Avery would agree to accompany me," Quentin returned. He couldn't disguise the glint of humor in his eyes as he smiled at Avery. He could see the wheels turning in her head and knew she could spit nails at him, but he suspected she would do the right thing.

Hunter whirled around and glared at Avery. When she didn't speak up, Hunter spoke for her. "I am sure Avery would love to join for your dinner to discuss an exhibition. Wouldn't you, Avery?"

Avery feigned a smile and said what was expected. Especially since her boss was present. "Of course, HLG would be honored to have someone of your caliber exhibit here."

"Excellent," Hunter said, leaving the duo. "I'll leave you to the details."

Once Hunter was no longer within earshot, Avery shot daggers at Quentin. "How dare you use my job as a weapon against me?"

"It was the only way I could get you to agree," Quentin fired back. "And who knows you just might enjoy a night out on the town with me."

"I doubt that," Avery replied, "but seeing as I don't have much choice . . . where should I meet you for this grand date?"

"Why don't I pick you up?" Quentin suggested.

"Oh no, I'm not giving you my address so you can show up at my apartment unannounced anytime you feel like it. No thank you." Avery crossed her arms stubbornly.

Quentin inched closer to her until their faces were inches apart. "Why must you challenge me on everything? Why can't you just let me be a man and pick you up like a regular date? Or do you get a kick out of being a shrew?"

Avery stepped back. What she didn't like was how vulnerable she felt whenever she was around him. "No, I don't get a kick out of it. You just happen to bring out the worst in me." She huffed. "But I suppose you can pick me up."

Avery sauntered over to the reception desk, giving Quentin a delicious view of her derriere as she switched in front of him. Avery quickly scribbled her number and handed him the Post-it.

Their fingers touched when he accepted the note. Quentin felt a spark and he was sure Avery had to feel too even though her expression belied nothing. "Thank you," Quentin replied. "That wasn't so difficult was it?" When she didn't reply, Quentin said. "I'll see you at seven."

Once the door had shut behind him, Avery exhaled. She hadn't realized she'd been holding her breath.

FOUR

S he told Hunter that she had a doctor's appointment and would be gone for the rest of the afternoon. Hunter wasn't too happy about it, but Avery could care less. She needed answers.

Woody didn't mince words. "Have you thought about why you're doing this?"

"Of course, or I wouldn't be here right now," Avery returned sarcastically. "I need to know my roots, if only for medical conditions. What if I have kids one day?"

"All right then, I'm not going to sugar coat this for you, Ms. Roberts. You have a long road ahead of you. Months, possibly years. Your original birth certificate that has your biological mother's name has been sealed, so if she hasn't registered with an agency or signed a consent form to release her identity it is going to be very difficult to find her. Do you understand what I'm telling you?"

"Yes." Avery nodded her head in agreement.

"First thing we need to do is gather as much information as we can," he said. "Such as your date of birth, the state you were born, the state where your adoption was finalized and, most importantly, what agency arranged your adoption."

"What do you mean date of birth? I was born on September 9th," Avery replied haughtily.

"Possibly, or perhaps you were born several days before?" he responded, "We just can't be sure. We have to check a few days before and after your birth date."

"Ohmigod!" Avery shook her head. *Even her birth date could be a lie?* "This is a nightmare."

"I know this seems daunting," Woody tried to calm her down, "but we may get lucky. You just never know in these situations. My advice to you is to talk to your parents and find out as much information as you can."

Her parents! They were the last people Avery wanted to see. Right now, she didn't want to have anything to do with them.

"I know you're angry with them," Woody said, "but they're our best bet."

"Thank you for your time." Avery stood and shook Woody's hand. She appreciated his forthrightness. "I'll be in touch." After she left his office, all Avery wanted to do was cry. She'd managed to maintain her composure even though she wanted to crawl up into a burrow like a groundhog and not come up for out spring. Whether she wanted to or not, she was going to have to contact her parents if she wanted details on her adoption, which was an unpleasant task and one she was not looking forward to.

AS MUCH AS Avery did not want to see either of her parents, she had no choice but to accept her father's lunch invitation mid-week when he called to mend fences. She hoped he would be able to shed some light on her adoption and provide cold hard facts that she could forward to her private investigator.

Woody Owen had called and thus far he'd found no record of a public adoption under her name in Manhattan, but he still had the entire state of New York to investigate as well as other states. These thoughts rumbled through Avery's mind as she met her father at the Lenox Room.

Prompt as always, Avery found him already seated at a table for two and dressed in a three-piece suit. "Avery, I'm so glad you agreed to see me." Her father stood up when she approached. When he leaned over to place a kiss on her cheek, Avery flinched as if burned and quickly sat down. It was hard to believe that the man she'd adored her entire life was not a blood relation. She'd always been Daddy's little girl. "I know you're angry with me and your mother," he began.

"Please, Dad." Avery put up a hand to halt him from continuing. "That's the understatement of the year. This isn't like the time you forbid me to go to the Rolling Stones and I didn't speak to you for a week. The wound is much deeper."

"I realize that, Avery," her father responded, "but I was hoping since you'd had a week to digest this information, you might be open to hearing our reasons why."

"What possible reason would you have for keeping the truth from me at this late date?" When he started to speak, Avery interrupted him. "Don't answer that. I bet you it was mother. Wasn't it? She was the one who made you continue this farce?"

"No." her father shook his head. "*We* both agreed it was best."

"Do you honestly expect me to believe that, Dad? I know Mother. I know what she's like. Heaven forbid I see her as less than the perfect wife and mother."

"That's true, she's not perfect," her father acquiesced. "She's human and as much as she'd like to think she's perfect, she's not because humans make mistakes."

"So that's it?" Avery asked, her voice rising. "That's it? I'm supposed to just sweep this under the rug to spare mother's feelings. Well, I won't do that Dad and you can't expect me to."

"I don't sweetheart. I just expect you to listen and have an open mind."

"Okay, fine. I'm listening." Avery settled back in her chair.

"Well . . ." her father started. "Initially, we had every intention of telling you the truth when you were old enough to understand."

"Did you ever try, Dad?"

Clayton Roberts shook his head. "Yes, we did. You

were eight and all the kids at school were questioning why you looked different from your mother and I."

"And as I recall," Avery replied, "you lied and told me that mother's great, great grandmother was mulatto."

"Yes we did, because by that point, we'd come to see you as our own flesh and blood, so much so that the truth began to matter less and less. And once we made that choice, there was no going back."

"That does not excuse the lies." Avery refused to let him off the hook that easily. "And now I'm old enough to understand, Dad. And want the whole truth and nothing but. Starting with names and places."

"Why?"

Avery didn't hesitate to answer. "Because I'm going to find my biological parents, starting with my biological mother."

"You can't!" her father said. "Avery, you can't do this."

"I'm not asking your permission," Avery replied. "I am going to find them with or without you, but I was hoping it would be the former."

"I don't know, Avery." Her father's head hung low. "If your mother ever found out this would hurt her terribly."

"I'm sorry, Dad. Really, I am, but this can't be avoided," Avery responded. "I need to know where I come from if nothing else than for medical purposes. What if I ever have kids someday? I need to know my family's medical history."

Her father sighed. Avery could tell he was wrestling with some internal demons, but without his help, it would be a lot harder for Woody to unearth the truth if ever and it would take a whole lot longer. "Well?" Wide-eyed, Avery peered into her father's dark brown eyes. "What's it going to be?"

After a long pause, he finally answered. "All right. I'll help you, but your mother's not going to like this." Clayton Roberts was certain of that fact. Veronica was going to hit the roof when she found out. And now was definitely not the time to tell her, she was already so distraught from this secret coming out. Clayton doubted she could take hearing that Avery was searching for her biological parents.

Avery nodded. "What I need to know is the name of the private agency you and mom used? And who oversaw my adoption." Avery pulled out a legal notepad, ready to take down some notes.

Over the next hour, her father informed her that Peter Gallagher, an attorney, had handled her adoption. Avery discovered she was not born in Manhattan at Columbia University Medical Center, Sloane's Women Center as previously told. She was actually born and officially adopted in New Hampshire. Her parents had picked her up hours after the delivery. Apparently, her biological mother hadn't wanted to see her for fear she might never be able to give her up. Avery was deeply hurt that she had handed her off to Clayton and Veronica Roberts without ever seeing her baby girl.

After lunch, Avery thanked her father for his openness and honesty. She knew it was difficult for him to do the exact opposite of what her mother would want, but Avery assured him that he'd done the right thing. She even responded to his second hug upon leaving and told him she'd be in touch if she found out any news. They'd both agreed to keep this information to themselves until Avery found out anything substantial. Why upset her mother unnecessarily?

Avery felt as if a gigantic load had been lifted and she could finally breathe again. When she called Woody on her way back to the gallery, he informed her that New Hampshire was a state which permitted adoptees over the age of eighteen to receive a non-certified copy of their birth certificate provided the birth parent placed a consent form on file. So Avery made a pit-stop by his office to copy her driver's license and fill out the necessary application form required by the Vital Records department, along with a permission note which Woody's secretary notarized that would allow Woody to receive the documentation. Once she gained access to her original birth certificate, Woody would have somewhere to begin his search.

When she arrived back at the gallery, a long, black stretch limousine was parked outside. Inside, she found Hunter with the owner of the gallery and from the looks of it, Hunter was giving Mr. Lawrence an earful.

"Hunter, Mr. Lawrence." Avery nodded to the two men.

"How are you, Ms. Roberts?" Henri inquired.

"I'm well thank you."

"I was just telling Mr. Lawrence the results of

Gabriel's showing the other night," Hunter said. "We did remarkably well, considering it was his first show."

Considering he was her find, thought Avery.

"Yes, we sold ten paintings," Avery chimed in.

"Eleven to be exact," Hunter corrected her. "We had someone stop by earlier today while you were at lunch and purchase another great piece."

Was that yet another dig at her? So she'd gone to lunch, what harm was there in that? Hunter was quite able to handle the gallery in her absence. He was director after all.

"That's wonderful news," Henri replied. "Keep up the good work." Henri patted Hunter on the shoulders. "I knew I made the right decision when I chose you to helm this location."

Avery despised the good ole boys network. She was quite capable of doing Hunter's job, if not better. Although Hunter was above her, Avery did all the hard work, but Hunter got all the glory. She supposed that was the downfall of being second in command.

"Well, I'm off to the airport for my fifteen-day Mediterranean cruise," Henri boasted. "I'll see you both in a few weeks."

"Enjoy." Avery put on a fake smile and waved as he left.

Once the door was closed, Hunter turned and faced Avery. "Where were you?" he asked. "That was an awfully long lunch."

"I had some personal business to attend to," Avery replied.

"You've had a lot of personal business to attend to the last couple of weeks, Avery," Hunter replied. "Are you looking for another position?"

"Why? Should I be?"

"I don't know, that depends," Hunter responded. "If you can't keep your focus on your job, then perhaps you should think about becoming a society woman like your mother. It's not like you have to work like the rest of us."

"How dare you?" Avery returned haughtily. "Just because I grew up privileged, does not mean I'm above hard work. Clearly, you know that by now."

"What I know is what I see. And what I see is that you've been distracted," Hunter replied, "and that's all I'm going to say on the subject." With that comment, he turned and strode away leaving his words dangling in the air. But Avery knew their meaning. Keep this up and she'd be pounding the pavement looking for a new job.

AVERY WAS nervous as she stood in the foyer of the two-bedroom Upper West Side apartment she'd lived in over five years, waiting for Quentin to arrive. She'd taken great care to dress for evening. She'd chosen to wear black trousers and a three-fourth sleeve multi-floral blouse as a jacket over her cami. It was smart and sophisticated.

When her doorbell rang, Avery's heart lurched. She willed herself to calm down and took one final glance before opening the door. Quentin was standing at her doorway looking calm, cool and collected while Avery's heart raced. Avery took a moment to let her gaze inch upward from his muscular chest to his chiseled face. His gleaming bald head was underscored by his intense eyes. His broad mouth broke out into a smile. "Avery," Quentin said.

"Quentin, you're right on time," she finally replied, glancing at her watch, but made no move to let him in.

"May I come in?" Quentin asked.

"Oh, of course," Avery stepped aside to allow him to enter her apartment.

Quentin wasn't surprised to find her apartment was as meticulous and in order as she. From the warm brown and beige tones to the cool earth shades, the apartment oozed sophistication and class just like the lady herself.

He stepped out onto her enormous balcony and found that her comfortable abode had a great view of Central Park

"Nice place," he commented on his way back in.

"Thank you," Avery replied. She was curious as to what was roaming through his mind as he fingered her Monet, Renoir and Degas prints that adorned her wall. He was probably thinking she was uppity and a snob.

"You must love the Impressionists," Quentin commented aloud.

"Yes, I like their use of short, thick strokes, the soft edges, the color intermingling and the way their paintings command your attention," Avery replied rattling on, until she realized Quentin was eyeing her up and down.

"What's wrong?" Avery asked. "Do you not like what I'm wearing?"

Quentin rubbed his goatee. "It's not that . . ." He paused.

"Then what?" Avery asked, exasperated. She thought she looked just fine. She was wearing Michael Kors after all.

Quentin chuckled at her tone. "It's fine if we were going to a fine dining restaurant, but for where we're going this evening, you are overdressed."

"Where are we going?" Avery asked again. Why was he being so secretive?"

"I've got tickets to the John Mayer concert tonight and I thought we'd grab a bite beforehand at this great Moroccan restaurant that I know."

"Moroccan?" Avery said haughtily. She'd never tried Moroccan food. All she knew was that they used a lot of curries and chutneys.

"Yes, Moroccan," Quentin replied, mocking her. "So, maybe

you had better go change and put on some jeans or something."

Aver glanced down at her outfit, "I think what I have on is just fine."

"I just thought you might feel more comfortable in some jeans or something at a rock concert. You know, less out of place, but it's your choice."

Avery thought about for a moment. He did have a point. She doubted her multi-floral jacket fit in with the rock crowd. "Give me five minutes," she said and scurried off to the master suite.

It took longer than five minutes for Avery to rummage through her closet because she couldn't remember what she'd done with the single pair of jeans she owned. She hadn't worn them in years and she could only hope they still fit.

Avery breathed in a big sigh of relief when they zipped up with ease. She glanced at her rear-end in the mirror. The jeans sure hugged every curve, she thought. Which is exactly how Quentin wanted it, she was sure. She replaced her jacket and shirt with one of Jenna's tops from her photo shoots. It wasn't really her style, but as Quentin was taking her out of her element it fit the occasion.

Avery breezed into the lobby and found Quentin perusing a magazine. "Will this suffice, your grace?" she asked, bowing in front of Quentin.

He smiled. Avery Roberts was certainly a ball-buster, but if she thought her sarcastic tone would send him running in the opposite direction she was wrong. He had a bet to win. He would show his friends that he was still a playa and like fine wine he had only gotten better with age.

Quentin rose to his feet and pulled Avery toward him. "Yes, that will do," he said, a mere inches from her face. The breath in Avery's throat caught in her throat and for a second she thought he was going to kiss her, but instead he released her and stepped away, leaving her bereft and wishing he had.

"Ready?" he asked.

"Yes." Avery huffed past Quentin, reached for her purse on the console in the foyer and preceded him out the door. Quentin smiled as he watched her swish out the door. He definitely liked the way she walked in those jeans. She'd been anticipating he was going to kiss her, but instead he'd wait. When she was panting for it, he would give it to her and give it to her good.

FIVE

Once they exited her building, Avery looked down the street for a taxicab, ignoring the motorcycle directly in front of her.

"You don't have to worry about one of those," Quentin said walking to the Harley parked directly in front of her.

"Why is that?" she asked.

"Because we're taking this," Quentin said, hopping on the back of the Harley.

Avery's eyes grew wide with fear as she walked to the curb. "Surely, you jest. There's no way I'm getting on that death trap."

"I'm not asking," Quentin said, handing her a Helmet. "Get on," He ordered.

"No," Avery shook her head.

"Don't make me get off this bike and physically put you on it," Quentin warned.

"I've never been on a motorcycle before. What if I fall off?"

"Then I guess you had better hold on real tight, now hadn't you?" Quentin chuckled. When Avery didn't move a muscle, Quentin got off and walked around the bike. "There's nothing to be afraid of. I'm a good driver and we have helmets to protect us." Quentin took the helmet out of Avery's shaking hands and placed it over her head.

"My hair," she said, when he snapped the helmet in place.

"It'll be fine." Quentin helped her onto the bike. "I promise I'll take good care of you," he replied as he hopped back onto the bike and turned on the ignition

"You'd better," Avery said, over the roar of the engine.

"Hold on," Quentin said as they took off down the road.

Avery held on for dear life. On the forty-minute drive from Manhattan to Parsippany, New Jersey, Avery prayed. She didn't know why she'd let herself be bullied into getting onto this contraption. She must be mad. She drew a long-overdue deep breath. They finally stopped at what appeared to be a small strip mall.

After they removed their helmets, Quentin grabbed her by the hand and said. "C'mon, you'll love this place. They have a live Moroccan band and belly dancers."

"Belly dancers!" Avery exclaimed.

The large wooden doors opened up into a warm atmosphere with hand-painted murals and fabric-draped ceiling, transporting her and Quentin into a fabulous Moroccan restaurant. The red and orange color scheme was a tribute to the many images she'd seen of Morocco and was nothing like any other place she'd ever frequented in New York.

They were ushered into a large open room where they were seated with other guests on banquettes strewn with ornate pillows. Avery was surprised that there weren't any tables. Handmade, intricately designed circular gold trays served as their tabletop. But before the meal was served, a waiter dressed in traditional Moroccan clothing brought over a *tasse* and a basin and set it on the small circular wooden table.

"What's that for?" Avery asked.

"It's for us to wash our hands," Quentin replied.

"Whatever for?" Avery queried.

"Because we eat with our hands," Quentin returned.

"Are you serious? That's completely uncivilized."

"It's the Moroccan custom. And as they say, when in Rome . . ." Quentin rolled up his sleeves.

Avery was surprised the restaurant was so crowded. She and Quentin had to sit at a small table with their thighs touching. It made her uncomfortable and she finally had to ask. "Why did you bring me here?"

"Because I wanted you to try someplace different. Take you out of your comfort zone."

"Why?"

"Because, my dear," Quentin tucked a loose strand of hair behind her ear, "you need to live a little."

"I am very cultured," Avery replied, somewhat offended.

"Why must you be so combative?" Quentin asked. "I just wanted to show you something different. Will you let me do that?"

Avery's eyes narrowed and he thought she was going to say no, but she smiled instead and said, "Yes. So, what are we having for dinner, because I'm sure you realize I have no idea what to order?"

What followed was a seven-course Moroccan meal that Avery would never forget. Quentin ordered items for them both to share, so Avery could try several of his favorite items on the menu. The first of which was a hummus appetizer served family style on a beautifully decorated platter.

While the waitress went to put their order in, Quentin used the time to learn more about Avery. He found she was a lot more open-minded than he thought and enjoyed many of the same things that he did. She had an affinity not just for art, but theater, literature, classical music and travel. She was well-traveled and had seen her share of the United Kingdom and Europe.

"Have you ever been to the Middle East?" Quentin inquired.

"No, I haven't," Avery replied. "I'm sure you have some interesting stories you could tell. I saw your Iraq photographs in TIME and they were amazing. You captured the despair and fear in the country."

"You have no idea," Quentin said. "The horrors and

atrocities that soldiers face when the go to war. . . It's brutal. No wonder many of them come back traumatized. My photographs only capture a second of the things they see and experience daily."

"Are you going back anytime soon?" Avery inquired.

Quentin shook his head. "No, as much as I like life abroad, I'd like to stay on American soil for a while. Plus, I kind of like the sights right here in New York," he said, staring at her from across table.

Avery blushed because Quentin was in no way hiding his obvious interest in her.

"Did I say something wrong?" Quentin inquired, inching closer to her.

"Uh, no," Avery replied. "It's just that you and I . . ."

"Have more in common than you realized," Quentin finished.

"No, what I was about to say is that we've lived totally different lives. I was brought up in a cocoon on Park Avenue, sheltered from the horrors of the world except what I see on the news. While you've seen them. Lived them. I'm sure that had to change you."

"Yes, it has," Quentin said and reached for her hand. "It's made me value life and all it has to offer."

Despite their differences, Avery felt a pull toward Quentin and had it not been for the waitress returning with their hummus appetizer, she might have fallen into his arms.

"What is it?" Avery asked, looking at the strange mixture.

The waitress answered. "It's a mixture of chickpeas, tahini, spices, and olive oil. Please try it."

"Here." Quentin reached over, grabbed a piece of flatbread and dipped in the smooth creamy mixture. He leaned over and put it to Avery's lips. "C'mon, don't be a chicken."

Avery took a deep breath and took the plunge. She bit into it and found the hummus to be surprisingly tasty.

"So, what do you think?" he asked.

Avery turned and smiled at Quentin. "It's not bad. Actually,

it's quite good."

"I'm glad you like it." He offered her another delicacy, *bastilla*. Crisp phyllo leaves powdered with cinnamon and confectioner's sugar to enclose the delicate, juicy filling of saffron chicken filling. It was completely sensual having Quentin feed her and not just because it was a mouth-watering blend of tastes and aromas, but because of the way Quentin looked at her. His gaze was a delicate caress across her face and Avery had to admit she enjoyed the attention.

They continued their meal with *harira*, a traditional lentil, Moroccan soup and a *tabouleh* salad of couscous, tomato, herbs and olive oil.

"I've never had anything quite like this," Avery had to admit when they were halfway through their entrée of slowly braised, baby lamb tagine served with saffron rice. "Thank you," she said when they ended the extravagant meal with a plate of fruit, pastries and a cup of mint tea.

"Don't thank me yet," Quentin replied when the live Moroccan band took to the stage. "The night isn't over."

Avery turned her head at the exact moment the belly dancer came sashaying into the room. Avery had no idea how she could shake and gyrate her hips with such ease. There was no way she could do that.

The dancer made her way around the room, asking several people to join her in the native ritual. When she made her way to their banquette, Quentin pointed to Avery. "She'd love to dance," he said.

"Unh, unh." Avery vehemently shook her head. "I don't belly dance."

"It is easy," the woman said with a large thick accent. "Come, I will show you." She pulled Avery to her feet and before Avery knew it the woman had wrapped a large piece of fabric around her hips.

As Avery rose, she noticed all eyes in the restaurant were on her as the Moroccan woman placed her hands on Avery's hips and showed her the movements in quick succession. Avery tried to follow suit, but found that belly dancing was not her forte. As she was sure Quentin suspected. When she turned and attempted to gyrate her body to the live music, she found Quentin's hot and hungry gaze fixed on her. Everyone in the restaurant clapped enthusiastically, trying to cheer her on as she gave belly dancing her best effort.

Quentin, meanwhile, was having great fun watching Avery give belly dancing her best effort. She wasn't inept, but she wasn't great either. If his friends could see her now, he highly doubted they'd be calling her an ice-queen. Despite her initial objections to his mode of transportation and choice of restaurant, Avery had come through like a real trooper. She'd shown that she could let down her hair and it made Quentin admire her for her courage.

Afterward, when she took a bow and returned to her seat, Quentin lied right through his teeth. "You were great."

"Liar," Avery said, glaring at him. "I'm going to kill you for this, Quentin Davis," Avery whispered in his ear.

"I look forward to it," he whispered back.

Two plus hours later, they left the Moroccan restaurant and headed back to New York.

An hour later found Quentin parking his Harley outside a small club. "John Mayer usually doesn't do small venues like this anymore, but because he got his start in places like this, he occasionally does one. C'mon, I think his set starts at ten."

He rushed Avery inside the small club. Avery wouldn't have suspected Quentin as the type to listen to acoustic soft-rock, more like R&B and hip hop. He continued to surprise her with his eclectic range of tastes.

The one and half-hour concert was on point. John Mayer sang his hits "Your Body is a Wonderland", "Why Georgia" and "No Such Thing". Throughout the concert, Quentin never strayed far from Avery's side. If she wanted a drink, he was right there. If she was grooving to the music, he was right behind her with his arms casually wrapped around her waist.

Quentin noticed that Avery didn't object when his arms encircled her waist. He was definitely making progress. When Mayer sung a really slow song, Quentin turned Avery towards him and they danced to the music.

"Thank you for wonderful evening," Avery said when they finally made their way back to Avery's apartment building. She hopped off the back of the bike and handed Quentin his helmet.

"You're welcome," Quentin said as he turned off the ignition. He swung his leg over the bike and locked both the helmets in place.

"Have a good night," Avery said.

She started to walk away, but Quentin said, "Wait!"

He spun her around and before Avery realized what was happening, his lips were descending on hers. They weren't unwelcome. Instead, they felt warm and inviting. His kiss was slow and addictive. It was like a drug she couldn't get enough of and needed a hit. When his tongue thrust hot and masterfully into her mouth and persuaded her into a duel, Avery responded with equal ardor. His hands meanwhile were scorching a trail as they skimmed her throat and the fullness of her breasts.

Afterward, she had to touch her lips because she felt as if he'd branded her his.

"You must have really needed that," Quentin said, when he released her from his embrace.

"Why do you say that?" Avery asked, haughtily taking a step backward. *Was he saying she was a bad kisser?*

"Because you kiss like you're making love. You have no

idea how erotic that is," Quentin responded. Quentin couldn't remember the last time a woman had kissed him with such abandon. There had been raw emotion behind that kiss and had surprised the heck out of him.

"Really?" Avery's cheeks turned red. No one had ever told her that before. In fact, most men had told she was too reserved and needed to let go. Perhaps, it was not her kissing technique, but the man himself who had brought out the passion in her? The knowledge made her pulse pound in her chest. *Could he hear its frantic beat?*

"Yes, really," Quentin smiled broadly. "If you kiss me like that again, I might have to take you back up to your apartment and ravish you all night." He was sure she had to have felt the bold evidence of his arousal pressed against her.

"Ravish me?" Avery laughed. "Quentin, do women really fall for lines like that?"

Quentin chuckled. "Hmmm." He rubbed his chin. "Sometimes. Yes."

Avery couldn't stop from grinning. She had a feeling he wasn't lying. There was definitely something about Quentin Davis that intrigued her more than any man had in a long time. She didn't want to be attracted, but there was no escaping his sheer magnetism. Or the fact that he was sexy as hell, funny, intelligent and cultured. "Thank you again, for a lovely evening, but it's late."

"Fair enough." Quentin leaned down and lightly swept his lips over hers. "Perhaps we can do this again another time?"

"Maybe," Avery replied. She didn't want to give a player like Quentin a big head and let him think he'd completely won her over. When in fact, he already had. "Good night," she said over her shoulder before entering her apartment building.

As the door closed behind her, Quentin shook his head. Avery Roberts was not going to cut him any slack. She was too stubborn to admit that she'd felt an attraction during that kiss just as much as he had. It had sure surprised the heck out of him. So much so, that now he wanted to see where this would lead and not just for the bet. Avery Roberts had piqued his curiosity. "Oh, there's no maybe, Avery," Quentin said. "We'll be seeing each other again real soon."

"YOU SOUNDED strange when you called and said we *had* to meet," Jenna said when she met up with Avery for dinner on Monday.

"Jenna, I wouldn't know where to start." Should she begin with the fact that she was adopted? Or that she was attracted to Quentin Davis?

"Why don't you try me? Talking it out might help," Jenna replied. "Is it your job? Did Gabriel's showing not go well?"

Avery shook her head. She wished it were as simple as that, but it wasn't.

"What then?"

She decided on the former. "I'm adopted."

"What?" Jenna's eyes grew wide. "Are you serious?"

"When I was helping my mother clean out the attic, I found my adoption papers and a copy of what turns out to be my amended birth certificate."

"No." Jenna was shocked. "Are you sure, Avery? I mean you're 33 years old. Why wouldn't they have told you before now?"

"I have no idea, Jenna. When I saw the word adoption written on those pages, I didn't know what to think, but they admitted it. They've lied to me my entire life."

"Oh Avery, I'm so sorry." Jenna leaned across the table and hugged her friend. "No wonder you haven't returned my calls. You must be so devastated. What can I do?"

"There's nothing that can be done, Jenna." Avery had had time to process the news and to take action, like finding her biological parents.

"Then a drink is definitely in order," Jenna replied. When a waiter walked by, Jenna tapped him on the shoulder. "Waiter, we'll have two apple martinis please." Jenna turned back around. "So, what's next?"

"I've hired a private investigator to look for my biological mother."

The waiter returned with two large martinis and placed them on the table. Avery was the first to reach for hers and sipped generously.

"How long does he think it'll take to find her?"

"Months, possibly years," Avery replied.

"I'm so sorry, Avery." Jenna reached across the table

and placed her hand over hers. "Let's talk about something else then, you know, take your mind off things."

"How about we start with my date with Quentin Davis?"

"Your date? Since when?" Jenna didn't recall Avery mentioning anything about a date with that gorgeous photographer.

"Since last night." Avery blushed, lowering her lashes.

"And?" Jenna was dying for details. She couldn't believe reserved Avery would actually go out of her comfort zone and date a hottie like Quentin Davis.

"Believe it or not, I had a lot of fun," Avery shrugged.

"What did you do?"

"We went to a Moroccan restaurant where we ate with our hands, if you can believe it?" Avery held up her pristine manicured hands. "My hands, Jenna," Avery said in disbelief. "And then he took me to a John Mayer concert."

"Wow, that sounds like an incredible first date," Jenna brow furrowed. "I'm jealous. So, how did it end?"

Avery closed her eyes for a moment and remembered the way his lips had moved over hers, coaxing a response from her. And the battery of sensations that assailed her at the slightest graze of hands on her breasts. Her eyes flew open immediately and she found Jenna openly staring at her.

"It must have been some ending!" Jenna replied.

"You have no idea," Avery smiled.

SIX

"So, are you ready to get back to work?" Quentin's agent Jason Morgan asked the following Monday when Quentin stopped by his office in Midtown for his next assignment.

"No, not really," Quentin replied. He'd rather gotten used to his carefree weeks off. "But I suppose I couldn't stay on vacation forever."

"No, you can't. Entrepreneur has been chomping on the bit for you to do a photo expose."

"Who's it on?" Quentin asked.

"See for yourself." Jason slid the manila folder across his desk. Quentin picked up the folder and flipped it open.

"Holy. . ." Quentin gasped. He was caught off guard by the contents of the folder. *Richard King* was his next assignment. Entrepreneur wanted him to follow King for a few weeks and reveal the man behind the billion-dollar King corporation.

"What's wrong?" Jason inquired. He was disturbed by his client's reaction to what was considered a great opportunity to showcase his talents.

Quentin stared speechless at the folder for several moments before handing it back to Jason. "I can't accept that job."

"Why the hell not?" Jason queried. "BLACK ENTREPENEUR will pay you a mint for your photographs."

Quentin shook his head. "I can't Jason."

"Until you give me a reason, Q," Jason replied, "I can't help you."

Quentin rose to his feet and walked over to floor to ceiling window. "You have no idea how messy this can get. Richard King is the man trying to take over the community center where Malik, Sage, Dante and I grew up. His corporation is trying to destroy the community."

Understanding dawned on Jason and he rubbed his chin thoughtfully. "So, your friends have come to you for help?"

"Yes," Quentin responded. "And I agreed to use all my resources to help stop this travesty. How can I do that if I'm spotlighting the very man who's a symbol of everything they're against."

"Because I already committed you," Jason replied. "I'm sorry Quentin, but I had no idea."

Quentin spun around and his dark eyebrows slanted into a frown. "Well, you're just going to have to un-commit me, Jason."

"I can't. I've already cashed the check. And anyway, it would be completely unprofessional. Quentin, I told you about this job weeks ago and you agreed. I can't go back and tell them you're not available. If I'd known this when you got back, I would have told them to look elsewhere. It's crunch time now."

Quentin understood where Jason was coming from. He was about the Benjamins, but money wasn't everything to him. He would be well off with or without this assignment. "There are any number of qualified photographers out there, Jason."

"They don't want another 'qualified' photographer, Q," Jason replied. "They want you. You're the best. And Richard King requested you," Jason added for good measure.

"Now, you're yanking my chain," Quentin replied.

Jason laughed. He couldn't kid a kidder. "Okay, perhaps that was laying it on a little thick, but go meet Richard King first and then if you decide you don't want to do the story, come back and I'll see what I can do."

"I don't know . . ."

"Perhaps if you met the man himself, you might be able to sway him."

"Away from a multi-million-dollar investment? I doubt that very highly, but I'll go," Quentin said, much to Jason's relief. He wanted to meet the tycoon who thought he could drive rough-shod over an entire community without any consequence or without anyone fighting back.

"Thank you," Jason said. "It'll all work out. You'll see."

Quentin shrugged. He highly doubted it. Matter of fact, he was sure the you-know-what was about to hit the fan.

When he arrived at the community center later that afternoon for his first photography session with the young men from the basketball court, Malik was there waiting for him. He'd arranged for Quentin to use one of the spare rooms.

"Quentin, what's up my brother?" Malik said, giving him a customary hug.

"Just here to show these young men," Quentin said, opening up the box of cameras he'd brought with him. He'd brought each of the boys a digital camera for their own personal use. He'd also brought some of his own equipment to show the basics of photography.

As the nine boys filed in, Quentin explained, "As you all know there are different types of cameras. Originally, everyone used a point and shoot 35mm camera. Now, with the exception of professional cameras, photographers have moved to digital photography that you can manipulate and edit. I've brought some with me."

"Quentin, you didn't have to do that," Malik replied.

"I wanted to." Quentin handed them each a camera.

Afterward, Quentin gave them each an assignment and asked them to take pictures of their family, friends, and community — anything of importance — and then he would bring his laptop in and share it with the rest of the group.

"I have to admit, Q, I wasn't sure you were going to come through," Malik replied.

Quentin frowned and stepped back. "Why not?"

"You're an important man. I wouldn't think you would have time to mess around with a bunch of kids."

"Well, you're wrong," Quentin replied. "Those bunch of kids were me. Could have been me if Mr. Webster hadn't stepped in. Listen, Malik, I know I've been away for a while, but have you really forgotten who I am?" The way Malik was talking it sounded like he had lost faith in Quentin.

"I'm sorry. I really didn't mean that how it sounded. I just meant that I'm happy those boys have a positive influence like you in their life. They need it."

"I'm happy to be here," Quentin replied. And he meant it. Even though he was between a rock and hard place professionally, he didn't intend to abandon the commitment he'd made to these young men.

"I HAVE GOOD NEWS," Woody said, when he called a few days later.

"You do —?" Avery's voice broke mid-sentence. She'd thought it would take much longer to receive an original copy of her birth certificate. She'd done some research on the internet and she'd read that it took adoptees years to find their birth parents. "Hold on a sec." Avery was in the middle of a sale and had to excuse herself before she could continue. She motioned to her intern to keep the client busy. "I'll be right back," she whispered to the customer and quickly rushed up the stairs to her office and closed the door. "Okay, go ahead."

"Vital records just faxed me over a copy of your original birth certificate," Woody replied.

"Wow!" Avery fell back into her chair. She couldn't believe her ears. It had only been a week. "It's as easy as that?"

"In this case, yes," Wood replied. "I'm as shocked as you are." He'd thought the process would take as long as four to six weeks. Avery was either really lucky or the office wasn't that busy.

"So, w. . . what's her name, Woody?" Avery asked with baited breath.

"Her name is Leah Gordon. "

"Leah." Avery mulled the name over in her head. "That's really pretty. What else does it say?"

"She was twenty-two years of age when you were born in Manchester, New Hampshire," Woody answered "I can fax you a copy if you like?"

"Uh, sure," Avery said uneasily. Did she really want to see the name her birth mother had given her before she handed her off to her parents?

"Sure thing, Avery. Putting it on the fax now." Woody handed his secretary the document. "Now that we know her real name we can begin the search. I'll start first in New Hampshire."

"But what if she wasn't born there?"

"Then we'll have to widen our search, which could

take much longer. But for now, let's run with the assumption that's she's a native of New Hampshire. And if so, then it's just a matter of following the trail of a woman with that name."

"How soon will you know something?"

"Don't know," Woody said honestly. "She could have moved or gotten married, changed her name or the name she gave on the certificate could be a fake, but as soon as I find out anything I'll be sure and give you a call."

"Thank you, Woody," Avery replied. When she hung up the phone, Avery experienced a gamut of emotions from excitement to absolute terror at the thought of a face-to-face meeting with her birth mother. Not to mention the fact that she and her father still hadn't told her mother yet. Avery was in the process of picking up the phone when a knock resonated on her door.

Avery rose and walked over and opened it. Avery tried not to show her displeasure at finding Hunter on the other side.

"Is it true, you just walked away from a sale?" Hunter inquired.

"Yes, it is," Avery replied. "It was just a few moments and I was just headed back down to finish the deal."

"Don't bother," Hunter replied. "I sealed the deal."

Avery sighed. Great. There went her commission because Hunter certainly wasn't going to give her a share in it. "Thank you."

"I hope that phone call was important, because almost cost this gallery a prime sale," Hunter replied.

"I'm sorry," Avery replied. "But the call was important."

"What is going on with you Roberts?" Hunter asked, eyeing her carefully. "You've been distracted the last couple of weeks. Is there something going on in your personal life? Do you need some time off?"

Avery didn't appreciate Hunter's inquest. "If there were, I wouldn't tell you," She responded. "My personal life is just that, Hunter. Personal. And no, I don't need any time off."

She tried to sweep past him, but he halted her arm. She glanced down at his hand and he quickly removed it.

"Fine, you don't have to tell me anything," Hunter replied in her ear, "but just know this, you had better get focused because you're on thin ice."

"I'll remember that," Avery retorted and shut the door to her office. Once Hunter had gone, Avery went to her fax machine and pulled off the copy of her birth certificate.

She held the piece of paper for several minutes in her hands before looking at it. She didn't know why she was so afraid to look. This is what she wanted, right? This is what she had hired Woody to do? So why was she so scared of seeing the truth in black in white? Avery didn't know why, but she wasn't ready yet.

Later that evening, Avery did what she'd been avoiding for weeks and stopped by her parents' home to speak with her mother, Veronica. It was time she told her that she was searching for her biological parents. As she opened the front door, Avery dreaded the task in front of her.

"Mom, Dad," Avery called out to her parents.

"Avery," her mother came from the back of the house and rushing towards her. "I'm so happy you came by. I've missed you so much. Knowing that you've been angry with me the last few weeks has been agony." Her mother gave her a big hug.

"Hello, Mother." Avery quickly patted her back and moved away.

"Darling, please come in." Her mother pulled her towards the living room and sat down on the sofa. She patted a spot next to her on the sofa. "Have a seat."

"Mother, this isn't a social visit," Avery said.

"I realize that, Avery," her mother replied. "I know you're very upset with me."

"That's putting it mildly," Avery replied. "Quite frankly, mother, I feel like I can't trust you. Which is why I'm here."

Her father walked in at just that moment. "Dad." Avery rose and accepted his kiss on the cheek. Why was it so easy for her to forgive her Dad but not her Mother? Avery wondered. She supposed it was because she'd always been much closer to her father than her mother. "I was just about to tell Mother the reason for my visit."

She watched his eyes widen with concern as he sat down opposite them. "Mother," Avery began, sitting back down, "I need to tell you something and I know this may hurt, but I felt I owed it to you to tell you where my head is at."

"Whatever is Avery, you can just tell me," her mother stated calmly.

Avery inhaled and released several long breaths before proceeding. "I've hired a private investigator to search for my birth parents and we received a copy of my original birth certificate today. Her name is Leah . . ."

"You did what!" Veronica Roberts rose to her feet.

"Mother, please," Avery began but her mother interrupted.

"How could you do this to me?" Veronica shook her head in disbelief. "To your Father. We've given you a great life. Haven't we?" her mother asked, grasping her by the shoulders.

Avery lowered her lashes. "Well, yes, but. . ."

"We're your parents," Veronica cried. "Not them. Where was this Leah person when you were crying? Or teething? Who fed you? Where was she when you skinned your knee?"

Avery could feel her mother's anguish and it caused the flood gates to open and tears to stream down her cheeks. She'd known it would hurt, but she hadn't realized just how deep the cut went.

"Veronica, stop it." Her father warned and stepped between the two women, but her mother was relentless.

"Was Leah at your first recital? Or your graduation? Why did you do this?" her mother shouted at her.

"Because I had to," Avery wailed, defending herself from her mother's tirade. "I didn't do this to hurt you,

Mother," Avery choked back the tears, "but I needed to know where I came from."

"Then go," her mother flung out her hand.

"Mother, please," Avery pleaded, "please don't be upset with me."

"Just go." Her mother swept past her and to the doorway, but not before leaving one final blow. "Go find your *birth* parents, but I promise you it will not bring you any peace. It will bring you nothing but pain. Just like the pain you've caused me," her mother said and ran up the stairs.

"What have I done," Avery said, lowering herself to the couch.

"You're doing what you have to." Her father took her side. "Your mother is hurt, but in time, she'll understand."

"I don't know if she'll ever forgive me for this, Dad," Avery replied. "You saw her."

"In time, she will." Her father came to her side and squeezed her shoulder. "You'll see. She's just hurt now, but give her time, she'll come around."

Avery could only hope that was the case.

AS QUENTIN WALKED UP to King Tower on Fifth Avenue and Fifty-Third Street, the building was as impressive as the man himself. After his meeting with Jason earlier in the week, Quentin had done a little research on Richard King. He was a prominent businessman with over five million square feet of prime Manhattan real estate and throughout Florida and California. He was an up-and-coming entrepreneur who could easily surpass Donald Trump, if given the opportunity. Quentin wanted to ensure that didn't happen, which is why he was here. He wanted to meet in person, the man, that symbolized the establishment and the very thing his friend Malik despised.

The inside of the tower was every bit as magnificent as the outside of the bronze-tinted fifty-story, glass tower. The use of marble, granite and brass throughout the complex and inside the four-level atrium which housed shops and cafés only added to its appeal.

As the elevator climbed, Quentin put on his game face. He would be professional and cordial. He didn't want Richard King to see that he had a hidden agenda. When the elevator stopped on the fiftieth floor, Quentin exited and walked up to the circular reception desk.

"May I help you?" she asked.

"Yes, I'm here to see Richard King," Quentin replied. "We have a two o'clock meeting."

"Certainly, just a moment please." She buzzed who he could only presume was Mr. King and while he waited she brought him a bottle of mineral water.

He hadn't asked for it, but he thanked her nonetheless.

After several short minutes, she said, "Follow me" and led him through the King Corporation swanky offices with plush carpeting and into Richard King's office. He was on the phone and motioned to Quentin to sit down.

Quentin took a seat with his photography bag and took a long hard look at Richard King. The man was not what he expected. Sure, he'd seen pictures, but in person

Richard King was short and didn't appear as looming a presence as the media made him out to be. In fact, from a physical standpoint, he looked rather ordinary. He was about five-foot nine, medium build and dark hair except for a pair of striking green eyes. He was wearing an Italian double-breasted suit that probably cost more than what Quentin made in a month.

"Mr. Davis, sorry about that," Richard King said, as he hung up the phone. "I'm sorry to have kept you waiting." He rose from behind his desk and came forward to shake Quentin's hand.

"Not a problem, Mr. King," Quentin said. "I understand you're a busy man." Once he was closer, however, Quentin noted that he had striking green eyes. If he were to take this assignment, he'd definitely want to get a close-up.

"When PR person told me about you shadowing me for weeks for an interview in BLACK ENTRE-PENEUR, I told him he must be mad. I have a huge development deal going right now," Richard replied, leaning against the front of his desk, "but some good PR never hurt right?"

"Right." Quentin went along.

"Why don't you join me for lunch?" Richard asked, standing straight and buttoning his jacket. "I have a business meeting that I must attend and you'll get to see me an action."

"Actually, I think that would be great," Quentin replied. "It's not problem for you?"

"Not at all," Richard returned. "I have nothing to hide."

Twenty minutes later, they were seated at the tower's restaurant while Richard met with a business associate. Throughout the hour-long lunch, Quentin watched Richard negotiate a deal. He was reasonable yet shrewd. Quentin entirely expected King to intimidate the lesser man, but by the end, Richard had his opponent thinking that he'd suggested the deal to begin with and not the other way around. Quentin had to admire his tenacity.

After the associate had left, Richard turned to Quentin. "So, what do you think?"

"I think you played your hand very well," Quentin replied. He was intrigued by the wealthy businessman. He wasn't nearly as ruthless as he thought.

"Well, it's all a matter of knowing the other person," Richard replied, looking him dead in the eye. "I knew he couldn't hold out for long. Getting what I wanted was inevitable."

"You're a very confident man."

"I wouldn't be where I am today if I weren't," Richard responded. "So," he rose to his feet, "how long do you think this expose going to take?"

"That depends on your schedule," Quentin replied. And as soon as he said the words, Quentin realized there was no backing out - he'd committed himself to this project. Malik was not going to be happy.

On his way to Dante's later that evening to deliver the bad news, Quentin decided he needed something pleasant to offset the unpleasant task that lay ahead of him. So, he dialed Avery's cell, she answered on the third ring.

"Hello?"

"How are you beautiful?" Quentin asked. He'd purposely waited several days before calling after their date. He didn't want to appear overzealous. If he came on too strong, Avery would bolt. If he wanted to win the bet, she had to be handled just right. And if he was lucky, those lithe limbs would soon be entangled in bed with his as he took them both over the edge.

Avery smiled on the other end of the phone. Quentin Davis was exactly the pick me up she needed after an emotional week. "Hello yourself," Avery responded.

"How's your week been?"

"Exhausting."

"How does dinner at my loft on Saturday sound?" Quentin wanted to get Avery on his turf and then maybe, just maybe he could break down some of the walls around that armor of hers. And pierce through that reserve. What better way than a home-cooked meal prepared by him to soften her up?

"Dinner at your place?" Avery wondered aloud. Was he trying to get her over to his place so he could seduce her? *Maybe you need a little seducing,* an inner voice said back. It sure had been a long time since she'd had that particular itch scratched.

"What do you say?"

"I don't know," Avery hesitated.

"I make the moistest lemon dill salmon you'll ever taste in your life."

Avery could just hear the little devil on her shoulder, saying go ahead, live a little. Enjoy Quentin Davis. Avery was sure he'd be fantastic in bed. That firm, chiseled body, that luscious mouth, Avery licked her lips. "Okay, okay. You don't have to convince me. What time should I arrive?"

"Seven?"

"Perfect. I'll bring the wine," Avery said before hanging up.

Quentin smiled as he closed his phone. He had Avery Roberts exactly where he wanted her. It was too bad the same could not be said for Richard King. Quentin hated to admit it, but King had impressed him with his negotiating skills and business prowess. He doubted Malik would see it that way. There had to be a happy medium, where he could do the job he'd been paid for and help his friend.

Quentin found the gang gathered at the bar nibbling on several of Dante's tapas.

"Q, join us," Dante said. "I've made some great new tapas that you'll love. How do some scallops in saffron cream, chicken croquettes, sautéed portabella mushrooms and some fried calamari with garlic mayonnaise sound to you."

"Sounds wonderful as always," Quentin said, sitting down at the bar. He avoided looking at Malik. "Dante, can I get a Corona?"

"Sure thing." Dante pulled out a bottle underneath the bar, popped off the top and handed it to Quentin.

"Thanks," Quentin said, hanging his head low.

"What's up?" Sage asked, eyed him strangely. "You look uneasy. Is this about your date with that upper-crust chick? How'd that go by the way?"

"Ah yes." Malik turned toward Quentin. "We've all been dying to hear the details. Or maybe you're keeping mum because you struck out?" he teased.

Quentin couldn't help but smile. Now here was a topic he was comfortable with. "Now, you should know me better than that Malik. A smooth player like myself never strikes out."

"So you hit a home-run?" Malik asked, raising an eyebrow.

Quentin paused for effect and his friends waited with baited breath for his answer.

"I knocked it out of the ballpark," Quentin boasted.

"You're still the man!" Malik raised his hand and Quentin hi-fived him.

"I knew it," Sage said, shook her head. "You are still every bit the playa you were when you left five years ago. So did you sleep with her?"

"I am too much of a gentleman to answer that question," Quentin replied. He had to keep some facts to himself. Despite her judgmental tendencies, Avery was a classy lady and didn't deserve to be bashed.

Dante surveyed Quentin's expression. "I just bet you did."

Quentin shrugged.

"Alright, well on to the next topic," Malik asked. "What are we going to do about the King Corporation? I was thinking of having a neighborhood meeting to gear up the community. You know get them excited."

"I think that's a great idea," Dante said.

"What do you think, Q?" Malik asked.

Quentin had been dreading this topic of conversation, but it was unavoidable. He was going to have to tell them that about his new assignment.

When Quentin didn't answer right away, Malik became suspicious. "Q, I asked you what you thought."

"Um, that sounds great," Quentin said distractedly. He

was trying to figure out how he was going to spin this news, but there was no way around it. He was just going to have to spit it out.

"Well . . .?" Malik was becoming annoyed at his lack of response.

Quentin took a deep breath. "Malik, there's something I have to tell you." He saw the worried look Sage gave him. For some reason, she'd always been able to read him better than Malik or Dante ever could. If he was lying she always knew.

"You see . . . when I got back my agent booked me an assignment and I gave him the go ahead, so he signed the deal on my behalf."

"And? What does this have to do with the King Corporation?"

"Yeah, Q. What's going on?" Dante asked.

"The assignment is Richard King."

"Holy . . .," Sage hissed underneath her breath.

"You have got to be joking?" Malik asked, glaring at him. Was this a cosmic joke? Surely, the universe couldn't be that cruel?

"Afraid not, Malik," Quentin responded. "You have to know I had no idea who or what the assignment was about. Or I would have never have given Jason the go-ahead."

"Can't you tell Jason you've changed your mind?" Malik asked, exasperated. "He is your agent, after all. He's supposed to get you out of sticky situations, especially since he's the one that created it."

"I can't do that," Quentin replied. "I wish I could, but

that would be completely unprofessional. Plus, it's not his fault. I should have asked before committing myself."

"But you can do it to me?" Malik inquired, folding his arms across his chest.

"Malik," Sage intervened and touched his arm. "Quentin said he had no idea. It's not like he set out to hurt you."

"No, but his keeping the assignment hurts not just me, but the center. A center that supported us," Malik pointed to the three of them, "our entire youth. But now that you're world-renowned you can't help the little people?" Malik shook his head in dismay. "I thought better of you."

"That's not fair, Malik," Quentin replied. "You know I care about the center and I will do whatever I can from the sidelines so that's it not a conflict of interest."

"Fair?" Malik yelled at Quentin and several patrons looked over at them. "None of this is fair. You know something, Q? you're nothing but a sell-out!"

"Sell-out!" Now Quentin was offended and stepped toward Malik. "How dare you call me that, Malik, after everything we've been through together? We're a family for God's sake."

"That's right. You've sold out to the establishment," Malik replied. "And now that you've gotten your piece of pie you don't care about anyone else. Well, thanks for nothing." Malik walked behind the bar and snatched his knapsack from underneath and headed towards the door. "I'll handle this myself. I don't need you, Q."

"Malik!" Dante grabbed his arm. "Don't leave like this, man. Let's just squash this."

"Dante's right." Sage came towards him. "I know you're angry, but we're all family." Sage looked at Malik and back at Quentin. Her eyes pleaded with them both to re-consider. "A dysfunctional one, but a family none-theless. Don't let business come between us."

"Let him leave if he wants," Quentin said, slamming his fist on the bar. "If you think so lowly of me, Malik, then you should leave before you say anything more that can't be taken back."

"Are you defending him?" Malik asked over Quentin's roar. "Because there's right and there's wrong and I would think you would know the difference."

Sage was taken aback at Malik's harsh tone. "Now you listen here, Malik Williams." Sage poked him in the chest. "I'm not taking any one's side. You're both my friends."

"Then fine," Malik replied. "If you're not with me, you're against me." He wasn't surprised Sage would take Quentin's side. He'd always been her favorite "And you, Dante? Where do you stand?"

Dante was pissed that he was being put in this posi-tion. He was between a rock and a hard place. He looked at both his long-time friends. "I'm with Sage on this. It's his job, Malik. I'm sure Quentin will do everything in his power to help. Won't you, Q?"

"Of course, I would," Quentin replied. "That goes without saying."

"Hmmm." Malik rubbed his chin. "For some reason, I

don't believe you, because lo and behold your word, Quentin Davis, is worth squat." And with that said, Malik stormed out the bar.

"Wow!" Dante said, turning to Quentin and Sage. "He sure is pissed at you, Quentin."

"I know."

"Well, what are you going to do to fix this?" Sage asked. "You've got to this fix this, Q. We can't let discord fracture our family."

"I wish I knew, Sage," Quentin replied, sagging into a barstool. Quentin had the sinking feeling that he'd made a huge mistake and destroyed a long friendship for money and his reputation.

AVERY DIDN'T REALIZE she was nervous about dinner at Quentin's loft until she felt her pulse beating at the base of her throat as the elevator made its way up to the fourth floor of Quentin's building.

It was just dinner and a movie, after all, but as she knocked on the door, she couldn't will her jittery stomach to calm down and when Quentin answered looking sexy and handsome as ever, her stomach instantly did somersaults.

"Looks like you've been busy," Avery said, nodding to the apron wrapped around his middle. "I brought a bottle of Riesling Hope that's okay?"

"Of course. I've been preparing a great meal for you," Quentin replied. "C'mon on in." He stepped aside to allow her to enter and shut the door behind him. Quentin immediately went back to the kitchen to check on the tapas he'd picked up from Dante's for appetizers that were warming in the oven.

Avery immediately loved Quentin's spacious and well-lit loft. The large windows facing the street, exposed brick and ductwork, stainless steel kitchen and state-of-the-art entertainment center made for a remarkable environment. There was one gigantic living area and restroom on the first floor and stairs leading to what she was sure housed the master suite. Photographs of his time spent abroad in Iraq, LIFE and TIME covers and various celebrity photographs lined his walls. It was no secret the man had talent and these photographs were a testament to it.

"What made you choose photography?" Avery asked when she finally made her way to the kitchen. She found him opening a bottle of Riesling she'd brought.

Quentin, twisted open the cork, "This will go perfectly with our fish." He poured generously and handed her a glass.

"White's fine," Avery said, accepting the wineglass.

"I had a great teacher." Quentin finally answered her question. "Someone kind and patient, who took a knucklehead like me under his wing. He taught not only the mechanics of cameras, but what to look for."

Avery smiled. "Sounds like he was good influence."

"More than that," Quentin said, seriously. "He was a father figure." Quentin openly staring at her. He was trying to figure her out. Avery Roberts was a beautiful woman who clearly had no idea just how beautiful she was. She didn't dress sexy to show off her assets even though she had the figure for it. Instead, she dressed conservatively, albeit in the best designer fashion. She was like a butterfly that was still trapped in the cocoon and needed to be let loose so she could be free and fly. Quentin wanted to be the person to release her from her inhibitions. There was a sexual being lying dormant underneath that smooth, polished exterior and carefully applied makeup. And Quentin intended to find out. But first, he would feed her and allow her to get comfortable before making his move.

He pulled a cookie sheet out of the oven filled with tapas and placed them on an oven rack on the bar to cool.

"Mmm, that smells delicious." Avery's mouth watered after seeing the decadent little bites. "Did you make those?"

"Afraid not. They're from my friend Dante's tapas bar."

"A tapas bar. That's a unique idea. Can I try one?" Avery asked leaning over the breakfast bar.

"Sure, but be careful, they're hot," Quentin said. He watched Avery take a delicate amuse-bouche in her mouth and savor the flavor. He was immediately aroused at the sight of her eating and the way her tongue flicked out to lick her lips was completely erotic. He could feel his manhood straining against the jeans he wore. It was good thing he was standing behind the bar and she couldn't see how hard he was.

"Wow!" Avery said. "If dinner is as good as that then I am in for a decadent feast."

"You most certainly are," Quentin groaned.

Conversation was stimulating throughout the entire meal of lemon-dill salmon, smashed parmesan potatoes and roasted asparagus that Quentin prepared. Avery was rather surprised by his prowess in the kitchen, but thoroughly enjoyed every bite. And she let him know just as much. "I hate to say it because I wouldn't want to give you a big head," Avery commented once they were seated on his leather sectional and enjoying a cappuccino and tiramisu, "but dinner was wonderful."

"I am glad you enjoyed it," Quentin rasped huskily, "you'll enjoy dessert even more."

Avery put her fork down and set her saucer on the table. *Was he coming on to her?* Because she'd heard a distinct sexual overtone in Quentin's statement and when she turned to him, Avery wished she hadn't. Those dark eyes of his were resting firmly on her and the intensity of his concentrated gaze made her tremble. He looked like a tiger ready to pounce and Avery had the feeling she was his prey. When he reached over and pulled one of the hairpins out of her hair and then the other, Avery balked.

"What are you doing?" she cried, trying to keep her hair in place, but it was no use.

"That's better," Quentin grinned at his handiwork. Now her glorious mane of hair had fallen generously to her shoulders. He'd been dying to do that since the first time they met. Avery was much too reserved for her own good.

"Why did you do that?" Avery said, running her fingers through her disorderly mane.

""You should wear your hair like that more often."

"Really?" Avery had always worn her hair up. She felt she appeared more professional that way. She didn't want to be the type of woman that played on her looks, but apparently she was wrong.

When Quentin saw the sour expression on her face, he'd realized he skipped a beat. "Listen, there's nothing wrong with wearing your hair up, just not all the time. You need to let loose, Avery," Quentin replied. "And I'm just the person to help you do it."

Quentin walked over to his entertainment center, he flicked on his CD player and immediately some up-tempo tunes flooded the air. Next, he opened a drawer and pulled out something, which Avery couldn't see from behind his back. She was shocked when he returned with a game of Twister.

"Are you serious?" She asked. Twister was a child's game.

"Yes, I am," Quentin replied, opening the box and pulling out the mat and spinner. "C'mon." He motioned for her to join him. "You'll see, it'll be a lot of fun." When she didn't move, Quentin rushed over and pulled Avery off the couch and towards the mat.

"You're crazy!" Avery couldn't resist laughing at Quentin's spontaneity. He continued to challenge her to venture outside her comfort zone.

"Yeah, I am," Quentin replied, "but I have a feeling

you like it."

Was she that transparent that he could he read her so easily? She didn't reply to his knowing comment, instead she said, "Spin the wheel."

Twenty minutes later, they were all tied up in a mess of limbs and arms. Somehow Quentin had maneuvered himself to be directly underneath her, while Avery had one hand over his head and her leg between his thighs. How had she found herself in such a compromising position? Quentin didn't make it any better because he was smiling at her like he knew something she didn't. He couldn't know she shared his attraction, could he?

When her hand needed to go underneath him, Avery lost her balance and so did Quentin, causing them both to tumble on the floor with her on top. Avery kept her head low, staring down at the curly hairs on his chest that were peeking out of the V-neck t-shirt he wore for fear she'd lose control if she looked at him.

Quentin tried to remain still to see what Avery would do next, but he just couldn't stop himself, he had to touch her. He slid his hands through her hair and brought her towards him until their faces where inches apart.

Quentin's gaze was fixed on her for what seemed like an eternity before he finally kissed her fiercely and passionately. Each second was filled with a building intensity Avery had never felt before. When he trailed his hands down over her body, smoothly and deliberately, Avery could feel her breasts firming and rising, she didn't know why until he rubbed the tip of his thumb over her nipple and she realized they ached for his touch.

"Oh yes," Sage moaned her pleasure.

And as the kiss deepened, he openly parted her legs, propelling her closer to him so she could feel the hard jut of his erection. Avery whimpered with raw delight at a familiar heaviness took over the lower part of her body.

His lips brushed her brow, eyes and cheekbone and then came to her lips. His tongue thrust deep inside exploring every inch of her mouth. While he suckled her tongue relentlessly, his hands shaped and caressed her ample bottom.

Before Avery could even register what was happening, Quentin was relieving her of her shirt and bra. He tossed them aside as if they were nothing but a mere inconvenience and then she felt his wet tongue on her naked breast. His teeth tugged at the dark nipple bringing to a ripe peak whilst the other cupped and caressed her other breast. She moaned her pleasure as he continued to take her to new heights.

When Quentin gruffly said, "Let's take this to the bedroom." It was like he'd splashed cold water on her face and waked her out of haze. Avery realized although she desired him greatly she wasn't ready to take their relationship to next level.

"Quentin, no," Avery pulled out of his embrace and sat up on the floor. She turned her back to him. Embarrassed that she'd let things get this far. She'd been so caught up in the moment, in the passion he'd brought out in her that it had scared the living daylights out of her.

"Why not? What's wrong?" Quentin asked. He'd thought everything was going rather well. He'd finally released the inner sexy beast in Avery and she'd responded him with an ardor he'd hadn't known she'd possessed. It hadn't just thrilled him, it had turned him on and he had a hard-on to prove it.

"Quentin, this is wrong." Avery reached across the floor for her discarded blouse and bra.

"How can it be wrong? When it feels so right?" Quentin asked. "I wasn't alone, I felt you responding to me."

"B . . . because," Avery stammered as she tried unsuccessfully to snap on her front-closure bra. "This isn't me. I'm not some sex-crazed maniac."

Quentin scooted over and snapped her bra in place for her. "Is that what you think we were?" Quentin asked, peering into her green eyes. "Because I strongly disagree. We were two grown adults acting on an attraction."

Avery slid one arm into her blouse and then the other. She was mortified by her scandalous behavior. *What must he think of her?* So Avery tried to clear the air. "I don't have casual sex."

"I am not asking you to have casual sex," Quentin said, "I just want you to allow yourself to let go. To lose control. Do you have to be in control all the time?"

Those were the words Avery remembered on the cab

ride from Quentin's loft. Why was it so hard for her to let go? She'd wanted Quentin as much as he wanted her. Her damp panties were a testament to that. So why had she run like a scared school-girl back to her apartment? She was a grown woman after all and shouldn't have been afraid of going after what she wanted. When had she become so afraid of taking risks? Avery vowed that if the opportunity presented itself with Quentin again she would not be so quick to run away. Instead she would take all he had to offer and then some.

EIGHT

Although Quentin enjoyed Avery's company the night before, he had more pressing business to attend to and that was making up with his long-time friend Malik, but try as he might Malik would not return any of his calls. He'd even stayed away from Dante's.

"What are you going to do to fix this?" Sage asked the next day when she met him at the bar the next day for a late lunch. The lunch crowd had long since left, giving them some time to talk.

"I don't know," Quentin said. "He won't return any of my calls. Do you guys have any suggestions?" Quentin looked back and forth between Sage and Dante.

"I'm afraid not," Dante replied. "When I asked him to join us to clear the air, he declined." Dante shook his head. "Malik is really blowing this way out of proportion."

"He's acting like child is what he's doing," Sage added. She didn't appreciate him putting her and Dante in the middle. "He wants us to take sides and I just won't do that." Quentin would never have taken the assignment had he known who the client was. Malik should respect Quentin's career just as he expected Quentin to respect the center. Sage knew what it was like to try to fight for the respect you deserved. She did it every day at the publishing company and she wasn't going to let anything or anyone get in the way of that. She knew that kind of passion.

"I appreciate your support," Quentin replied, "but I don't want it at the expense of your relationship with Malik."

"No, Quentin," Sage said, swiveling around in her barstool to face him. "I will not be railroaded. I know what it's like to have to put your career first."

"So that's what you think I'm doing? Putting my career above my friendship with Malik?"

"That's not what she's saying," Dante interrupted. "She's saying that she understands that your career is dependent upon your professionalism."

"Exactly. It wasn't like you did this on purpose and that's what Malik is failing to see. He's being really pigheaded." Sage was furious with him. She'd called him half-a-dozen times and he'd refused her calls too.

"Yeah, but you know Malik . . .," Quentin said. His voice trailed off as he stared down at his glass. Ever since they were teenagers, Quentin had known Malik to be somewhat angry. They knew the abuse Malik had endured as a child and now he was trying to make up for all the wrongs against him by helping other people and children in need. That's why he took as a personal affront that Quentin was taking this case. "I should just tell Jason that they need to find another photographer."

"And what will that do to the career you've spent years to build?" Sage asked. "You know as well as I do that you're hot right now. You've got to ride this wave until it ends. Or do you want to go back to being poor?" Sage remembered all too well what it was like growing up with nothing except the hand-me-downs she was given to wear. She refused to go back and she doubted Quentin wanted to either.

"But he's family!" Quentin rubbed his bald head. He was torn between a fierce need to survive at all costs and between doing the right thing for a friend who was a brother to him.

"I do and eventually he'll get over it." Sage was adamant.

"You do remember what happened that time Tiffany asked me to the spring dance even though Malik had a thing for her?" Dante inquired. "Malik wouldn't talk to me for weeks."

"And *eventually*," Sage emphasized, "he got over it."

"I appreciate all of your advice," Quentin said, "and I'll do it your way and give Malik a little time to cool off. If that doesn't work I'm going to go see him and squash this myself."

"Whew!" Dante wiped his brow. "I'm glad that's over

now I can get back to the kitchen and get started on the dinner menu."

"So, now that Dante's gone," Sage said, "let's get down to basics. What's up with you and the art gallery woman? How's the bet going?"

Quentin thought about it for a moment. Avery Roberts had become more real to him than just some bet. She was a vibrant woman and one he wanted tremendously. "Everything is going just fine," Quentin said.

Sage peered into Quentin's dark brown eyes. "Are you holding out on me, Quentin Davis?"

"Of course not, Sage," Quentin said, swigging back his beer. He could be honest with Sage and tell her what was on his mind without fear of razzing like Dante or Malik. "We had a great first date at that Moroccan restaurant I took to you when I visited last year."

"Oh yeah." Sage nodded as she remembered the palace. "Great ambience."

"It got even better when Avery belly-danced for me," Quentin smiled.

"Get out! You got Ms. Priss to actually loosen up and belly-dance?" Sage chuckled. "Wonders never cease!"

"I sure did *and* she rode on my motorcycle," Quentin commented. "And did I mention that she came over to my loft for dinner last night."

"And?" Sage knew there was more to the story.

"And nothing," Quentin answered. "We had a great time."

"I've got to hand it to you, Quentin," Sage replied,

sipping her red wine. "You have a way with the ladies. I'm sure she has no idea what's in store for her does she?"

Quentin rubbed his goatee. What he had in store for Avery Roberts was not only going to please her but be pleasurable for the both of them. Had she not run away the other night, Quentin was sure they would have become intimate. He was curious to see what lie beneath that cool exterior. If last night was any indication, he was in for a wonderful surprise.

"JENNA, I WANT TO MAKE A CHANGE," Avery said when she met up with her best friend in the foyer of the Dominic Sabatani Salon the following day. Avery was impressed by the opulent furnishings and artistic details. The interior director had left nothing to change from the floor-to-ceiling windows to the Venetian style glass chandeliers.

"A change? What kind of change?" Jenna asked excitedly, rubbing her hands together. "Are you finally going to give me the chance to make you over?"

"Yes," Avery stated unequivocally. "It's time I change my image. You know, spice things up."

"What brought this on?" Jenna asked.

"Well . . .," Avery started. "I'm not one to kiss-and-tell, but things between me and the photographer have heated up."

Jenna's eyes grew wide. "How heated did they get?"

"We nearly made love on the floor of his loft," Avery said and couldn't resist smiling.

"Nearly? Why didn't you finish?" Jenna inquired. "If it were me with Quentin Davis, wild hogs wouldn't have been able to pull me out of his bed."

Avery shrugged and slid her fingers through her hair. "I don't know, Jenna. . . Call it what you want. Fear. Propriety. Lack of confidence. I don't know. Even though I wanted him as much as he wanted me, something stopped me. And life is too short. I want to be free to live my life and not be tied down by expectations."

"And you think a makeover is going to instantly change that?" Jenna asked, snapping her fingers. "Because I doubt that. It will give you self-confidence, but my dear the rest is going to be up to you."

"Well, let's get to it," Avery said, standing up from the reception bench.

"Great!" Jenna said, "What stylist did they book you with?"

"Star."

"No, no." Jenna shook her head. "That will never do." Jenna walked over to the reception. "Let me talk to Edward, please. Tell him it's Jenna Chambers."

A few minutes later, Dominic Sabatani swept into the reception area and kissed both of Jenna's cheeks. "My dear, it's so good to see to you," Dominic said.

"You too, Dominic," Jenna replied. "But my friend here," she motioned to Avery to stand up and come over, "is in need of your help and must, must, must be cut by your hands. I can't entrust her hair to anyone but you."

"You are too kind," Dominic replied. "But I'm booked, ma cherie." Dominic glanced at Avery's unflattering ponytails and bangs. "And your friend is in need of a complete makeover."

"Dominic, you have always been able to squeeze in a Wilhelmina model. You just have to do this. Consider it a favor for me."

Dominic's eyes narrowed. "Alright, I'll cut her during my lunch hour, have Sonya wash her and then I'll finish the style afterwards. But she's going to need Blair for makeup and Emily nails to complete the look."

"You are a lifesaver, Dominic," Jenna said. "And I am in your debt."

"And one day I'm going to collect on all the favors you owe me," Dominic chuckled and then glanced down at his watch. "Be back by noon." And just as quickly as he came in, he was gone in a flash.

"Sure thing," Jenna said to his retreating figure. "Prepare to say goodbye to the old Avery." Jenna walked toward her and grabbed her by the elbow. "Because a new world awaits you." One Avery was looking forward to.

Two hours later, Avery was stunned at the sexy woman staring back at her from the golden-leafed mirror. Dominic Sabatani had worked a miracle and transformed her former bland hair and bangs into a work of art. He'd used his shears to create a chic, razor cut, keeping most of her length, but adding volume with varying lengths. Avery was very pleased with the results. Blair had applied the right shade of foundation, eyeshadow, blush and lipstick revealing a sultry sexy woman with arched eyebrows that Avery hardly recognized.

"Bella," Dominic said when he stopped over on his way to receive another client.

"She does look amazing." Jenna nodded her head in agreement. She'd stayed with Avery throughout the makeover to be sure she achieved the right look.

"Thank you," Avery beamed.

"Come back again."

"I most definitely will," Avery said, rising from the silk-draped stool. She took a moment to admire herself one final time before turning to Jenna. "So, are you ready for some shopping? Because I can't have a new hairdo without new clothes to match?"

"Go shopping, girlfriend, you don't ever need to ask," Jenna replied and together the two of them joyfully bounced right out of the salon. They finished their day with stops at Macy's and Bloomingdale's, which left Avery's wallet bare by the time she returned to her apartment with several bags tucked underneath her arm. She was nearly inside when her phone began to ring. She quickly fumbled in her purse for her keys and once she found them inserted them into the lock. Immediately, she dropped her bags and made a dash for the phone.

"Hello," she said out of breath.

"Avery, are you all right?" Quentin asked from the other side of the phone.

"Oh, I'm fine. I just came in from shopping with Jenna," Avery replied.

"Listen, Avery about last night," Quentin began.

"Stop," Avery interrupted him, "if you were about to apologize. None is required. We both know I wanted you as much as you wanted me."

"Then what happened?"

"I don't know. I guess I froze. Can we take it slow and see what happens next?" Avery didn't want to remember what a fool she'd been to leave his loft.

"Yes, we can," Quentin replied. "How about a picnic on Saturday in Central Park?"

"Sounds great," Avery said, smiling through the phone. "I'll bring all the trimmings." After she hung up the phone, Avery took a moment to admire herself in the hall mirror. Come Saturday, Quentin Davis would meet the new and improved Avery Roberts, one who wasn't afraid to take a risk.

ALTHOUGH QUENTIN COULDN'T WAIT for the weekend to come, he still had to work to do, namely shadowing Richard King bright and early on Monday. His press secretary had arranged for Quentin to follow him to several important functions over the next couple of weeks, all in an effort to get Quentin to photograph King favorably as a rising entrepreneur and not a ruthless tycoon. The first of which was a weekly business meeting with his top executives to go over impending deals.

Quentin had been allowed to set up his equipment in the boardroom prior to the start of the meeting, so that he'd have a good angle to shoot King. As the executives started to pile in, Quentin focused the camera lens toward the head of the table. The meeting was in full swing for several minutes before Richard finally arrived. Immediately everyone at the table rose as if he were a king. Quentin snapped a photograph.

The flash caused Richard to look in Quentin's direction. "Mr. Davis, I'd forgot you were going to be here. Have you been introduced?"

"No, I haven't," Quentin replied. Not that it mattered to him. He liked to be in the background when he was working. Then he could capture the unexpected.

"Everyone, I'd like to introduce world-renowned photographer, Quentin Davis. Mr. Davis is going to be shooting a spread on me for Entrepreneur magazine. Please give him your full cooperation." The executives nodded their heads.

Hour later, Quentin had several interesting shots. Several of which were as Richard pulled off his jacket, rolled up his sleeves and loosened his tie to get down to business. Quentin was rather surprised that he didn't let his right-hand man do all the work for him. Instead, Richard seemed apprised of all the pressing deals going on in his multi-million dollar enterprise and wasn't afraid of getting his hands dirty. Quentin had expected a tyrant; instead he got a man who listened to his top executives' ideas and suggestions yet offered a firm hand to guide them in the right direction. Quentin couldn't help but be impressed by Richard's fair dealings. So, why is it the man could treat his employees fairly on one hand and destroy a community on the other? Quentin just didn't understand it.

When the conversation turned to the Harlem deal, Quentin's ears perked up. The architect was led in with a mock-up model of the proposed site which would house residential condominiums, office, retail and several restaurants. It was an ambitious deal and one that apparently Richard King was up to his neck in financially. When it came to discussion of how to convince the storeowners to sell, as much as Quentin wanted to listen in, he felt it was unethical to stay and tried to excuse himself. "If you'll excuse me," Quentin said and started toward the door.

"No, stay," Richard said, rising from his seat and shutting the door. "This is a new project King Corporation has in development. I'm very excited about it. Please stay."

Quentin thought better of it. He didn't want to hear of the underhanded methods they were willing to use to run poor people out of their community, but he had no choice, so he stayed put.

One of his top executives began. "Richard, our main opposition is the community center. That center is the lifeblood of the community. Without its support, this project is doomed."

"How do we get it?" Richard asked, rubbing his chin thoughtfully.

"The director and community center board adamantly

refuses to even hear our offer. We've proposed re-building the center in another location down the street. The new building would have all the latest computer and hi-tech medical equipment available, but they will not listen."

"Perhaps I should go by the site myself and talk with the director," Richard replied. He remembered a time when he'd frequented Harlem in his youth. It held a lot of dear memories for him, ones he would never forget.

"Are you sure that's a good idea, Richard?" his executive replied. "I can handle this."

"I'm sure you can, but I think I'll stop by there later in the week. Quentin, you should join me and take some photographs."

Quentin hated that idea. What if Malik saw the two of them together? That would only further infuriate his dear friend.

"As you wish," the executive sat down clearly defeated.

"Don't worry, you're still in charge of this deal," Richard replied, "but before we get too far financially into this, I want to know we've got all the bases covered. With that being said, I have another meeting to attend to. Meeting adjourned."

Richard swiftly headed to the door, leaving Quentin to wonder just how far Richard King would go to seal this deal. And what did that mean for the community center and Malik?

•   •   •

WHEN AVERY CAME to work on Monday morning with her new haircut and wearing a black pencil skirt, crea lace halter and short black jacket, even Hunter had to comment on her appearance.

"Avery, what did you do to yourself over the weekend?" Hunter replied.

"I had a little makeover at the Dominic Sabatani salon," Avery replied.

"Well, you look great," Hunter said glancing at her and just as soon as he said something he nice he took the words away with a sorry comment. "I'm sure your new look will do wonders for the gallery."

"Excuse me," Avery said, folding her arms across her chest. "Are you saying that my former appearance brought down the gallery?" She'd always dressed appropriately.

"No of course not. Don't be so touchy." Hunter touched her shoulder. "You've always been the utmost of professionalism. I merely meant that"

"That I wasn't all that attractive before?" Avery replied. "Thanks a lot, Hunter. You really have a way with compliments." Avery turned on her heel and walked away.

"I merely think you're more appealing to a buyer now," Hunter said to her back as she stalked up the stairs to her office. Avery could just ring that guy's neck. Everything he said was lanced with venom.

Avery was going through the mail and her paperwork, when she stumbled upon the fax from Woody. Why had she left the certificate at work instead of taking it home? Perhaps because she was running away from the unknown as she had done with Quentin on Saturday night. Maybe it was time she confronted the truth head on rather than fear it. Slowly, Avery slid the coversheet off to reveal her Certificate of Live Birth. Avery learned she was named Baby Gordon. Had her birth mother been too busy to give her a name? She was born at 1:54 p.m. on November, 3, 1974 in Manchester, New Hampshire to Leah Gordon. But what Woody hadn't revealed over the phone was that her birth father's name had been left blank. *Had her birth mother not known who her father was? Or had she been so ashamed at having a child out of wedlock that she'd left his name off on purpose?*

The certificate claimed her mother's birthplace was Manchester and listed an address, but was that the truth? Had her birth mother given a fake address and birthplace so that she'd never be found? It was the first time Avery thought that maybe she wouldn't want to be found? But why not? How could a mother not want to know the child she gave away was all right? Had lived a good life? Her birth mother would want to meet her, Avery told herself. She was a positive about it and when Woody found her they could take steps to form some kind of relationship. Avery wasn't sure what that would be, but she would not expect the worst. Instead, she would hope for the best.

MALIK HAD NEARLY a week to cool off before Quentin stopped by the community center for his Monday photography session with the boys. When he arrived, he found that the room Malik had promised was being used.

Furious, Quentin stormed into Malik's office. He was a meeting and sitting at a circular table with several people when Quentin burst in. "Malik, I want to talk to you *now!*"

Malik glanced in Quentin's direction and turned to his colleagues. "If you'll all excuse me, I'd like to talk to Mr. Davis," Malik replied. They rose from the chairs and quickly exited the room.

"Quentin, don't come here starting trouble. Because that's the last thing I need right now. Why don't you just go back to your Soho loft or Rome or Paris or wherever you feel comfortable these days and leave me to deal with real life issues."

"Malik," Quentin walked up to his best friend and looked him dead in the eye, "I know you may be upset with me, but that is no reason for you to take it out on those boys. I gave them my word."

"Your word," Malik laughed derisively. "Your word isn't worth the paper it's written on. I believe you gave *me* your word that you would help the center and as soon as it wasn't convenient for you or might interfere with your next big paycheck you bailed. Leaving me holding the bag. Well you know what, Q? I won't let you do that to those boys."

"*I* am not doing anything to them," Quentin's voice rose. "You're the one that's punishing them. I know they enjoyed that lesson and I was eager to see what they'd come up with."

"Well, don't bother," Malik replied. "We don't need

you. Mr. Webster was kind enough to volunteer and take your place. Since unlike you, he cares about this center."

"That's not fair, Malik," Quentin shook his head. "I want to be here and I gave you a generous donation last week."

"Money? Sure we could use that anytime." Malik was pissed. "But what we needed from you was clout and influence and since you can't be bothered, then consider you services no longer needed." Malik reached into his desk and pulled out the check Quentin had signed and held it out to him. "Here take it. We don't need your blood money."

Quentin was crushed. That really stung. "Keep it," Quentin shook his head. "Whether you approve of my actions or not, the center needs it." Quentin started towards the door, but then stopped. "I'm really sorry you feel this way, Malik. I came here today to try and make amends. We've been friends for a long time. Hell, you've been a brother to me when I had no one. You and Dante have gotten me out of more scrapes than I could remember. But if this is the way you want, then I'll honor your wishes and stay away."

"I would appreciate that," Malik replied and turned his back on Quentin. "Now could you please close the door on your way out."

Quietly, Quentin shut the door behind him and walked out of the center and perhaps out of Malik's life for good.

NINE

There wasn't a cloud in the sky on Saturday when Avery and Quentin shared a picnic on the Great Lawn in the middle of Central Park. The green grass, colorful trees and blooming flowers made for a romantic setting for their third date.

Avery had prepared a delicious picnic basket from her favorite delicatessen with cold-cuts, pasta salad, cheese, crackers, fruit and a nice bottle of wine to wash it all down with.

Quentin met Avery at Bethesda Terrace by the fountain. Quentin was surprised when a stylish woman walked toward him and kissed him on the cheek. "Avery?" Quentin looked her up and down and took in her skinny capris that showed off her narrow waist, a halter tank which revealed a generous swell of breasts and quarter-length wrap. She sure didn't look like the Avery Roberts he knew. Sheer foundation adorned her face while mascara and shadow tinted her eyes, but once she smiled back at him and he made contact with those brilliant green eyes of hers, Quentin knew he had one and the very same. "Wow!" He drew a shallow breath.

"So, do you like?" Avery asked, spinning around so Quentin could get a full view of the new and improved Avery Roberts complete with new haircut, make-up and a brand-new wardrobe thanks to Jenna.

Quentin grinned. "Yes, of course. You're stunning!"

Avery couldn't help but grin from ear-to-ear. That was exact the response she was looking for. "Thank you."

"What prompted the change?" Quentin asked. He wasn't sure what to make of this new Avery. He'd looked forward to exploring a new side of her, but the Avery standing in front of him looked very sure of himself.

"You did," Avery answered honestly. "You asked me to loosen up and let myself go and this is it." Avery placed her hands on her hip.

"Well, you definitely know how to let yourself go," Quentin said, taking the picnic basket from her. They strolled through the mall underneath the green canopy of overhanging trees to the Great Lawn. Quentin laid out the blanket he'd brought with him and sat down. Quentin offered his hand to Avery to assist her in joining him on the blanket. The look in his eye was unmistakable to Avery. He liked the new Avery. No, make that he wanted the new Avery. The knowledge sent a little shiver up and down her spine.

"So, what did you bring?" Quentin asked, looking over

her shoulder as she unpacked the picnic basket. "Oh a little of this, a little of that." Avery smiled knowingly. "Here pop this open." Avery handed Quentin a bottle of white wine and bottle opener. He quickly uncorked the bottle and leaned over to pour the wine into the plastic flutes she'd brought.

Quentin's mouth watered when she laid out the appetizing spread. For the next hour, they indulged in stimulating conversation along with their cold-cuts, pasta salad and fruit. Afterwards, they both got comfortable and laid out on the blanket to soak in the sun's rays. Quentin was amazed at how comfortable he felt with Avery. He used the opportunity to get an unbiased opinion about his new assignment and its effect on his relationship with Malik. "He's terribly upset with me, Avery, and I don't know how to make it right."

Avery was happy when Quentin confided in her. It showed that their relationship was progressing. "I'm sorry to hear that," Avery said. "Doesn't Malik understand that it's just assignment? It's your career on the line."

"I'm afraid not," Quentin said, turning to face her. "He sees that if I'm not with him, I'm against him. He only sees things in black and white."

"And life is in shades of grey," Avery replied. Boy, had she learned that. It would be so easy if she could just hate her parents and turn her back on them, but she couldn't because she loved them. And although she was angry that they'd kept the truth from her, she knew that deep down they loved her. And that's what she told Quentin. "I know he's angry with you now, but he still loves you, Quentin," Avery said, stroking his cheek lightly with her hand.

That tiny, but tender action warmed Quentin's heart and caused him to reach over and pull Avery toward him and brush his lips across hers. She tasted of strawberries, ripe and sweet. "You taste so good," Quentin groaned.

"So do you," Avery whispered and kissed Quentin again.

"Come with me." Quentin pulled Avery to her feet. "Since you are feeling carefree what better way than a ride on the carousel."

"Surely you jest," Avery laughed. "The carousel is for kids."

"Who says?" Quentin asked.

After a short walk, he was helping her onto the back of a hand-carved horse and joining her on the horse by her side. "You are so crazy!" Avery yelled when the carousel took off.

"And you love it!" Quentin replied.

Avery laughed. Because he was right. She loved that about Quentin. He was fun and exciting. He kept her on her toes and she never knew what was coming next.

When the three-and-half minute ride was over, they strolled over to the polar zone at the zoo to watch the polar bears, harbor seals, penguins and sea lions. When Quentin reached out to hold her hand, Avery didn't object. She was having the perfect date, one she'd never had before. They were admiring the sea lions when Avery felt a raindrop. "Did you feel that?" she asked.

"Feel what?" Then Quentin felt it. Rain. Why did it have to rain when they were having such a perfect day? "C'mon, we better head out of here." He picked up the picnic basket on the floor and grabbed her hand. But before they could even make it out of the zoo, they were caught in a torrential downpour.

"Ohmigod!" Avery said as the rain ruined her brand-new haircut and soaked her clothes.

"Don't you live around here?" Quentin said, squinting at Avery through the rain.

"Yes, I live on Seventy-ninth and Central Park West."

"Great, let's get out of here," Quentin said. They quickly ran through the park and once they made it Fifth Avenue, Quentin hailed a cab. Luckily, a yellow taxi pulled up immediately to the curb and they hopped inside.

"Can you believe that weather?" Quentin asked. One minute it was bright and sunny and the next it was raining cats and dogs.

"No," Avery replied, shivering. "Look at me. I'm a mess." She glanced down at her ruined outfit

"You're beautiful," Quentin responded, pushing the damp hair out of his way so he could see her face. "And you're shivering." He leaned over and rubbed her shoulders to warm her up. Avery instantly warmed and the touch of his big strong hands against her heated flesh. When the cab stopped in front of her building, her doorman graciously came out with an umbrella though it would hardly do much good since they were both soaking wet.

"Thanks, Mike." She nodded to the doorman. An air of sexual tension permeated the ride up to her apartment. Quentin was staring at her with such naked hunger that Avery thought she would combust if he didn't touch her soon. The prolonged anticipation was almost unbearable. Thankfully, the elevator stopped soon and they entered the comfort of her apartment.

"I guess we should get out of these wet clothes," Avery said, once Quentin shut the door and dropped the picnic basket.

"Yeah, I think that would be a smart move," he responded, looking over at her seductively. Heat flared bright in his eyes. When Avery went to remove her jacket, Quentin said, "Here let me help with you that."

He swiftly closed the distance between them and her hands trembled slightly when he slid the jacket off her slender shoulders and leaned down to delicately brush his lips against her damp skin. Avery shuddered, but she didn't stop him. Instead, she helped by throwing her arms in the arms, so he could pull the damp halter off her body. She was wearing a bra. She didn't need to.

When Quentin's eyes boldly raked over Avery's bare breasts and up to her face it caused his libido to kick into high gear. He dipped his head and nestled his face between her breasts. He teased one nipple with generous laps of his tongue until it turned into a rocky peak. And when he was done with one breast, he feasted on the other, until she was so overwhelmed, she whimpered aloud and moisture settled in her panties.

"Oh yes."

Quentin took her moans to mean she enjoyed and looked up to search her eyes for any apprehension and when he found none. He swept her into the circle of his arms and claimed her lips. His mouth covered hers hungrily. His kiss sent spirals of ecstasy through Avery and she returned it with reckless abandon. She wanted to be closer to him to feel his hard body against hers. When they finally parted, Avery reached down and removed his damp shirt out of his jeans. She looked up at him as she unbuttoned each button slowly.

Quentin thought he was going to go mad with desire if she continued the slow pace. When she reached the final button, he ripped the shirt off and tossed it across the room. Then he swept her up, weightless into his arms, and marched towards her bedroom. She was surprised he remembered since she'd only shown him once. When he gently deposited her on the bed, Avery sat up. She didn't want to be a bystander; she wanted to be an equal participant.

"Come here," Avery ordered, beckoning him with her index finger.

Quentin smiled. "Aren't we eager," he said. He was enjoying this new self-confident Avery and allowed her to unzip his jeans.

"Yes, I am," Avery replied, pushing them down his legs. "I want you, Quentin Davis, and I intend to have you."

"Oh you can have me, Avery," Quentin replied. "The

question is can you handle it?" he challenged, stepping out his jeans and joined her on the bed. Now it was her turn. She wasn't nearly naked enough. He reached for the zipper on her capris.

"Oh I can handle it," she looked smiled seductively at him. She lifted her hips allowing him easier access to remove her capris. Her sexy panties followed the same path and quickly hit the floor.

Quentin spread her legs and brought his warm mouth to that intimate part of her and hovered, leaving Avery eager for him to know her fully. And when she finally felt the entry of his teasing tongue, she lifted her bottom of the bed, but he grasped her hips firmly in his hand and tongued her, devouring her greedily. A spasm engulfed her and a scream escaped from her mouth. As she came, her womanly scent inflamed him while her moans were music to his ears causing him to lean down and reach for the foil packets in his pants. He'd decided to have some with him after the way things had heated up after dinner at his loft. He quickly completed the task protecting them both.

Moments later, was taking one nipple in his mouth and licking and sucking and teasing until she was whimpering for more. That's when he shifted his body over hers and slid inside her warm, her heat, her fire. He began thrusting deep inside her, branding her his. He possessed her like no other man had. They were in sync as he pumped inside her. She was swept up in a tidal wave of pleasure and he followed her by throwing his head back and letting out a shout. She wrapped her legs around him as they both tumbled over the edge, together.

"Wow, that was pretty incredible," Avery said when she finally caught her breath and was able to sit upright.

"You're telling me," Quentin replied. "I didn't know you'd be such a tigress." She'd responded so openly and honestly. Giving of herself that it threw Quentin for a loop.

"I didn't know I was capable of that kind of passion," Avery responded. "Quite frankly, I've never cared for sex. I could take it or leave it. Other men never made me feel the way you make me Quentin."

Quentin stared down and her and gently stroked her hair. He appreciated her forthrightness. She was being so open and honest it made him feel guilty for not doing the same. He'd bet his friends that he could get Avery into bed and now that he'd won, he'd felt he'd lost something too. Because if he ever told her about the bet, she'd never forgive him.

"You know being with you, Quentin, has changed me. I feel more alive and open to new experiences."

"Such as . . ."

"I don't know," Avery shrugged. "Whatever you'd like to explore." And that's exactly what they did for the new few hours. They took the time to explore the other's body and find out their likes and dislikes. Avery was even open to new positions she may not have tried in her previous sexual relationships.

After a short nap, they snuggled up under the covers

with the rain still beating outside. Avery felt so comfortable with Quentin that she could talk to him about anything. She was quiet, debating whether to discuss her family when he scratched her head. "Is everything okay?"

Avery nodded.

"Something's on your mind, though?" Quentin said, intuitively. "Whatever it is you can talk to me. I haven't forgotten when Jenna said at Blue Note that you had a lot to deal with. My shoulder is here for you to lean on."

"Thank you, it's just that I don't know where to begin, Quentin," Avery replied. "The last few weeks have almost been more than I can bear."

"Try me," Quentin said pushing several pillows backward and opening his arms to Avery. She scooted upward and into the crook of his arm. When she did, he wrapped his arms tightly around her letting her know he was a safe haven.

"A few weeks ago, I was helping my mother clean out the attic when I stumbled upon a chest."

"What was inside?"

"Some documents I was never supposed to see. Quentin," Avery turned to face him, "I found a legal document that revealed I was adopted."

"Adopted, wow!" Quentin said. "And from your tone I take it they never told you."

Avery shook her head. "I'm thirty-three years old, Quentin, and they never said a word. They kept the truth from me and the only reason I found out was because I was curious at my mother's reaction when I stumbled on it.

They tried to explain, but how can they? My whole life has been a lie."

"I'm so sorry, Avery. This must have come as quite a shock."

"I just don't understand how they could do this. They had every opportunity to tell me. Quentin, I've always known I was different. Felt it somewhere deep inside that I didn't fit in with my family now it all makes sense."

"Maybe they were afraid. Because once they didn't tell you, the lie had become so great they couldn't come back from it."

Quentin could understand how her parents felt, because he felt the same way right now.

"That's no excuse," Avery returned. "I know this isn't a black and white issue, Quentin. I'm just so furious with them, I could spit nails."

"Avery, I know you're upset, and you have every right to be, but your parents love you. Do you even realize how lucky you were to have been adopted? To have someone to love, care and protect you?" Quentin was upset that she was taking her family for granted.

"I know I've had a privileged life," Avery began, but Quentin interrupted her and grabbed both sides of her face.

"You were extremely lucky, Avery. You should be thankful, some people aren't so lucky."

"I know, I know," Avery shook her head. "You must think I'm extremely spoiled."

"No, what I think is if you had lived a day in my shoes, you'd realize how fortunate you are."

"Why? Did you have a terrible childhood?" Avery realized she'd never heard Quentin mention his family. *Why hadn't she noticed that before?*

"If you count growing up in foster care from age thirteen until I was legal," Quentin replied, "then the answer would be yes."

"You grew up in foster care?"

"Yes. Malik, Dante, Sage and I grew up in foster care. Because we were in our teens, we were never adopted. So as you can see, Avery, you lucked out. A wonderful family took you in as a baby and nurtured and loved you like parents should. My friends and I were not."

"Quentin, I had no idea. And here I am going on and on about how upset I am with my family. But I have one."

"And you're entitled to be upset. I'm not trying to take that away from you," Quentin responded. "I'm just trying to give you a little perspective.

"I appreciate that," Avery smiled hesitantly, "but if you don't mind my asking, how did you end up in my foster care?"

"Well. . ." Quentin paused. "My mother pretty much moved around from man to man, so my grandmother raised me. When she passed away from a stroke, I was put into the system."

"What about your mother? Did they even try to look for her?"

"They did, but it was as if she disappeared off the face of this earth."

"Did you ever try to find her?"

"No, I didn't," Quentin answered honestly. "I guess I never wanted to. If she had wanted me, she would have called or come back to check on me. She never did." The anger in Quentin's voice over his mother's abandonment caused Avery to keep quiet about the search for her own biological mother. She wanted to share the news with him, but she doubted he would understand her desire to find the mother who'd given her up at birth, especially when he was coming from a place of such pain and hurt.

"Well, it looks like we both have some parental issues to work out," Avery said.

"Yeah, I suppose so. I guess that's what makes this disagreement between Malik and me so profound. He's my family, Avery." Quentin's voice caught in his throat. "Malik, Dante and Sage are all I've got."

"Not anymore," Avery said and leaned up to kiss him full on the lips. "You've got me."

"Do I now?" Quentin asked.

"Yes." Avery slid closer until her pert breasts were pressed firmly against his hairless chest. "Matter of fact, you can have all of me, right here and right now."

"Hmmm." Quentin groaned. "I think I'll do just that," he said, flipping her over until she was pinned underneath him. He ravished her with his mouth, tongue and hands until they both fell off to sleep.

TEN

"It was the best sex I've ever had," Avery told Jenna over lunch on Wednesday. She'd been so enraptured with Quentin over the weekend, she hadn't had a chance to call her and tell her about their date. They'd spent Sunday in bed exploring each other's likes and dislikes.

"Hallelujah!" Jenna shouted and several people turned to stare at them. "You finally slept with that gorgeous fox. Good for you, Avery."

"I'd never felt such passion" Avery said, twisting her napkin in her hand. "It was so intense." It had been much too long since she'd felt so wanted, so needed, so desired.

"So he rocked your world!"

"More than that, he turned it over on its head." Avery ran her fingers through her hair. "He's reawakened me sexually, Jenna. I didn't even know my sexuality was dormant until he lit a fire under it. And I don't understand. We're polar opposites."

Jenna smiled, "You know the old saying, opposites attract."

"I suppose." Avery shook her head in amazement. "I just don't know where this is headed."

"Where do you want it to lead?" Jenna inquired.

"Honestly, I don't know," Avery answered. "We're so different. I'm reserved. He's carefree."

"But you share common interest too, right? Like art? He's a photographer, I'm sure he appreciates it too. Why don't you stop making excuses for why you don't want to be with him and grab life by the balls and run with it? Don't be so afraid."

"I'm not," Avery huffed. "We became lovers, didn't we?"

"And now you're trying to find a reason to end things," Jenna replied.

Avery hated that her friend knew her so well. She was way out of her comfort zone with Quentin, and if she weren't careful she could fall hard for him. That knowledge scared her half to death. "I'm not," Avery lied. "I intend to enjoy Quentin for as long as the feeling's right."

Jenna shrugged "Sure, you say that now, but I have feeling that there's a lot you're not saying."

Avery grinned. If she only knew.

QUENTIN MET Richard and his assistant across the street from the community center for his meeting with Malik. He didn't know why he'd agreed to drive over here with Richard. Maybe it was some warped need to show Malik that he would go through with the assignment whether he liked it or not.

"Can't you just see some high-rise condominiums here, a movie theater and some specialty eateries?" Richard's chest puffed at the idea of his latest deal. He didn't wait for Quentin's response, but instead he charged across the street and toward the center entrance. Despite his reservations, Quentin had no choice but to follow behind him.

"I'm Richard King and I'm here to see Malik Williams."

"I will let him know," the receptionist replied.

Quentin couldn't help but notice the sour expression that crossed her face. She, too, must know that this man had the power to bring the center down. "Please have a seat."

A look of disdain came across Richard's face as he glanced across the room. Quentin doubted he wanted to sit down in his Gucci suit in the modest lobby with standard brown chairs that looked as if they'd been sat in one time too many. "Thanks, but I'll stand," Richard said.

Quentin folded his arms across his chest and steeled himself for Malik's reaction to his being there.

Several minutes later, Malik came bursting through the door. He was about to speak when he saw Quentin standing in the corner. "What are you doing here?"

"Do you two know each other?" Richard asked, looking back and forth between the two men.

"No," Malik replied. The look of disappointment he

sent Quentin's way caused him to lower his head. "I meant you."

"I believe my assistant made an appointment," Richard returned coolly. He wasn't put off by Malik's brusque tone.

"Doesn't matter," Malik responded, throwing back his dreads. "Because I have nothing to say to you, Mr. King. Trust me when I say that I'm speaking for the Children's Aid Network and the community center. They are not for sale. Not now or in the future."

"Mr. Williams, I understand your apprehension, but if you'd give me a chance to explain." Richard snapped his fingers at his assistant to hand him his portfolio. "I can explain the benefits my complex would bring to the community." He extended the portfolio to Malik, but he ignored it.

"So, what are you? The Great White Hope that's going to save the community?" Malik laughed bitterly. "I don't think so. You've got an uphill battle ahead of you, Mr. King, because we are not going to go quietly. Good day" Malik glared at Quentin one final time before storming back into the office.

Richard was stunned. No one had ever walked out on him. The director hadn't even given him a chance to go over his plans.

"I told you," His assistant said from his side. "Yes, well, I will never give up," Richard said, heading toward the door.

Quentin stayed put. He wanted to tell Malik that although he was there in a professional capacity, he was still behind the center one hundred percent, but he doubted Malik would even listen to him.

"Quentin?" Richard turned to him. "Are you coming?"

"Uh, yes," Quentin said, grabbing his photography bag off one of the chairs and following him and his assistant.

"The meeting did not go as I anticipated," Richard said once they were outside.

"Did you expect anything less," Quentin responded, turning sideways and staring at Richard. He'd come to the center since he was a child and would hate to see it demolished to make room for a multimedia complex and condominiums.

Richard spun around at Quentin's sharp tone. "I take it you don't approve of my new development?" He'd noticed that the photographer hadn't been particularly pleased when he told him they were driving to Harlem this morning. Matter of fact, he'd made every excuse in the book not to join him.

"Approve?" Quentin asked. "I think it's a travesty to this community." He was relieved to finally get the words off his chest.

Richard didn't understand Quentin's hostility to his new development. "I'm willing-to relocate the center a few blocks away."

"So that makes it okay to tear down a landmark?" Quentin asked. "That center," Quentin pointed to the building, "has been there for nearly fifty years. The community depends on it. Yet somehow your money-making trumps that?" Once he'd spoken his frustrations out loud; Quentin realized just how unprofessional he'd acted. As a photographer, he was supposed to be objective and take pictures, Hut this assignment hit too close to home. He'd lost all objectivity.

"Well, well," Richard chuckled. "I'm glad to see you're not a yes man and speak your mind." Richard despised cowardice. "I can appreciate that"

"Even though you don't agree with it," Quentin returned facing Richard.

Richard smiled. "No, I don't. My development will benefit the community and bring in precious revenue and jobs."

"After you've displaced all the storeowners and residents," Quentin snorted. "Sounds great."

"How do you know so much about this area?" Richard replied, eyeing him strangely.

"Because I grew up around here." Quentin didn't offer more details.

"And yet you're doing an assignment on me. When it's clear you don't approve of what I represent. Why?"

"I made a commitment and I'm honoring that."

"A man of integrity." Richard smiled. In his line of business, it was hard not to be jaded. "I don't see many of those in my world. And I appreciate your honesty, Quentin Davis." Richard extended a hand, which Quentin reluctantly shook. It was just too bad Quentin couldn't say the same about him.

• • •

SAGE SHOWED up unexpectedly at Quentin's apartment later that evening. He'd been standing near the window remembering the evening he'd spent making love to Avery. He'd enjoyed giving her pleasure and watching her intense reaction as she came. She was wanton and sensual and just the type of woman he wanted in his bed. So why did making love to her throw him into such a panic? Because he was accustomed to being in control, but he'd gotten completely lost in her. He was struggling with the possibility that any woman could make him feel any sort of emotion, but Avery had. She'd gotten to him. Him? A man who didn't do commitments.

"What are you doing here?" Quentin asked when she walked in carrying a bottle of wine and a large foil package.

"I brought dinner from Dante's," Sage replied, holding up the food. He walked the tin over to the kitchen and started opening cabinets to remove several plates. "Since you haven't been to the bar in over week and haven't returned any of my calls, I thought I'd better come by and check on you."

"Yeah, well," Quentin said, shutting the door. "I thought perhaps it was better to keep a low profile, that way Malik would come by and not feel uncomfortable at my presence."

"That's very magnanimous of you," Sage replied, pulling a large spoon out the drawer underneath the counter and lading the plates with spaghetti carbonara. "Now open that bottle of wine."

Quentin walked over to the kitchen and yanked the bottle away from her. "You know, you didn't have to do this, Sage." Quentin uncorked the bottle and poured two glasses.

"I know I didn't but you've been a little too quiet all week," Sage added.

"Have you ever thought there was a reason I hadn't called?" Quentin replied, handing her a glass. Suddenly, his mind raced with illicit thoughts of how incredibly responsive Avery had been in bed and the little sound she made when he was buried deep... He was getting in too deep. He should pull back before there was no turning back.

"Oh?" Sage's eyes widened. "Have you and Avery grown closer?" When Quentin remained mum, Sage got her answer. "I see. So, she's the reason you've abandoned your friends."

"One week does not abandonment make. Avery and I are two adults who shared an incredible weekend. Is anything wrong with that?"

"Of course not," Sage replied. "But if I recall, you weren't supposed to get involved. Just get the ice diva to melt."

"Thanks, Sage." Quentin already felt guilty about gaining her trust under false pretenses. He'd pursued her relentlessly and now what? Guilt gnawed at his insides.

"I'm not trying to make you feel bad," Sage said.

"I know, I know," Quentin replied. He hadn't been looking for anything serious either, just a little fun. But in the short time he'd known her, she'd been real and honest with him. She'd let her guard down and opened up to him about the fact that she was adopted. He'd even trusted her and told her about his rocky childhood. He couldn't remember the last time he trusted a woman with his feelings, but he had with Avery.

"If you didn't feel anything, I'd think something was wrong," Sage replied to Quentin, "but you do." Sage walked around the counter and peered at Quentin. "So something tells me that Avery's come to be more than you than you envisioned. Are you falling for her, Q?"

"Of course not." Quentin denied it even though deep down he knew it to be a lie. "I'm not a relationship kind of guy. I don't do commitment."

"You're lying," Sage fired back. "You've developed feelings for her, but you're afraid to admit it."

"I'll admit that she's not the ice queen I originally thought she was. She's warm, kind and passionate. Extremely passionate, but that doesn't mean this is going anywhere. Matter of fact, I've won the bet so if I wanted to, I could move on."

"But you don't want to, do you?" Sage queried. "You're going to continue seeing her, aren't you?" Quentin didn't answer. Sage patted his back. "It's okay, Q. It'll be our little secret. Enjoy Avery. You deserve all the happiness you can get."

· · ·

"I DIDN'T FIND any matches in New Hampshire. So, I expanded my search to include the East Coast and I located several matches."

"That close?"

"Yes, I figured given the times back then your biological mother probably went to Manchester to give birth to avoid controversy in her hometown."

"And?" Avery held her breath. She was sure there was more that Woody wasn't saying and she was almost afraid to know the answer.

"I've found her Avery."

Suddenly, all the air went out of the room and Avery grasped for her chair to avoid passing out. "You . . . you found her?" Avery pulled her chair underneath her.

"Yes. She lives in upstate New York, in Buffalo to be exact," Wood replied. "I have an address for you, if you want to write it down."

"Give me a minute, okay? To catch my breath. This comes as quite a shock." Avery hadn't expected Woody to find her biological mother so quickly. Once she had a few moments to compose herself, Avery finally asked. "What can you tell me about her?

"Well," Woody paused. "Her name is Leah Johnson now. She's a married and a mother of three."

"So, she has more children?" Avery replied.

"Yes, two boys and a girl."

"I see."

"Avery, I know this must be upsetting for you. But your mother was only twenty when she had you and wasn't ready to be a parent. She waited to have children until she was in her early thirties."

"How old are they?" Avery inquired, "My half-brothers and sisters, that is?"

"The oldest boy is twenty-one, the youngest is nineteen and your half-sister is sixteen."

"And her husband?"

"A prominent surgeon. He's well respected in the community. Leah's a homemaker."

Avery felt sick to her stomach. Sounds like her biological mother had a wonderful life after she'd given up her first child. "Thank you, Woody. I really appreciate everything you've done."

"It was my pleasure. Now if you have a pen and paper, I can give you her address and phone number."

Now that the information was right in Avery's grasp, she hesitated to reach for it.

"Avery?"

"Oh yes, go ahead." Avery jotted down Leah's address and phone number in Buffalo.

"Give me a call, Avery. I'd like to know how it goes."

"Sure, Woody," she said as she hung up.

When her fingers began dialing Quentin's cell phone, it surprised Avery that he was the first person she wanted to confide in despite the fact that she hadn't told him about her search. To tell him that she had mixed emotions about finding out the identity and location of her biological mother. "Quentin, it's Avery."

"Is something wrong?" Quentin asked because he could tell she was upset.

"I need to talk to you. Are you going to be home later?"

"Yes, whatever you need. I'm here."

"Great, I'll see you after work."

Avery walked through work in a daze. She had mixed emotions She'd even ignored Hunter's snarky comments. She was thankful when the clock struck five and she could leave the gallery.

When Quentin slid open the door to his loft, Avery rushed into his arms. She wrapped her arms around his neck so tightly, Quentin could hardly breathe. "Baby, what's wrong?" Quentin asked.

"Everything," Avery replied, finally releasing Quentin. She headed to his sectional couch and took a seat.

"Talk to me," Quentin said, closing the door and coming toward her. "What happened?"

"I hired a private investigator to find my biological mother?"

"I see. Why didn't you tell me before?"

"Because I thought you might be upset. You told me be to be thankful for the parents I do have and I didn't want to appear ungrateful."

"Avery, you're welcome to your feelings. I would never deny you that. My experience and your experience are totally different. I knew who my mother was. She just chose not to care. On the other hand, you have no idea who she is. If I were you, I would want to know where I came from to."

"You would?"

"Yes." Quentin smiled and stroked her cheek.

Avery nodded. "Well, I know now." Avery attempted a smile. "Woody found her, Quentin, and I don't know what to do. When I started this, it was more of an issue of entitlement. I had a right to know who she was, but now that's it's here," tears welled up in her eyes, "I'm scared, Quentin. I'm not sure if I should have opened Pandora's box. She has a whole new family now."

"You don't have to *do* anything with this information, Avery," Quentin replied.

"Why do you say that?" Avery queried. "Is it because you never searched for your mother?"

Quentin was slightly offended. "One thing has nothing to do with this other. I merely meant that you can take some time and digest all of this."

"And, what aren't you saying, Quentin?"

"I'm cautioning you, Avery." Quentin scooted closer to her on the couch. "I don't want you to get hurt or be disappointed. Because as you said, she has a whole new life now. She may not want to include you."

"Or it could be the reverse?" Avery replied, struggling to be optimistic. "She may want to get to know me."

"I would love for that to be case for you, Avery, but what if isn't?" Quentin tried to be the voice of reason. He'd hate for Avery to have her hopes dashed.

Avery shook her head. "I don't know, Quentin." Avery's voice caught in her throat. "Yes, I could get hurt, but I also need to know where I come from. I don't want to spend life staring at strangers to see if someone looks like me. For once, I'd know where I fit in."

Quentin understood more than she knew. He remembered all too well what it felt like to be an outsider. He'd felt like one as a teenager, but once he'd made friends with Malik, Dante and Sage, it didn't seem to matter as much anymore. He'd found a safe haven, a place to call home. That's what his friends were to him. They were like home. "Come here," Quentin said, leaning back and sinking into the cushions. Avery scooted closer until she was sandwiched between his big strong thighs with his solid chest as her pillow. When she rested her head on his chest, Quentin softly stroked her hair. "I'll support you in whatever you decide," Quentin said, leaning down to brush his lips against her forehead.

"Thank you," Avery looked up at him, "because I doubt my mother's going to feel the same way. Do you know she hasn't talked to me in weeks? She was so upset when I told her I was searching for biological mother. Imagine how she's going to feel when I tell her I not only found her, but I'm contemplating meeting her?"

"I doubt she's going to take it very kindly," Quentin replied.

"You're telling me. She's going to fly off the handle. But I can't not tell her. I already accused them of keeping secrets. How would it look if I did the same?"

"Would you come with me when I tell her?" Avery asked. "She's got this big charity Vegas night with Nora Stark and her crew on Saturday night and I go every year.

If I didn't, she'd get suspicious. I figured I could tell her after the gala."

"Are you sure you want me there?"

"Only if you want to come," Avery replied, sitting forward. Perhaps she was moving too quickly and he was feeling smothered at the idea of commitment. They hadn't really discussed where they were headed or if this was just a casual thing. "I mean if you have other plans, I completely understand. We're not a couple or anything."

"It's not that, Avery," Quentin replied. "I would love to join you. I just thought you might want some privacy to talk to your parents."

Avery breathed a huge sigh of relief. So, he wasn't trying to blow her off. She sure hoped so. She didn't want to be the only one feeling like a connection.

VEGAS NIGHT at the Carlyle was all glitz and glamour when Avery arrived with Quentin. Dressed in a tuxedo and with a button clip shirt, Quentin outshined every man in the room in Avery's eyes. And he smelled even better. "Are you nervous about meeting my parents?" Avery inquired.

"No, should I be?"

"Maybe, I haven't brought a man to meet them in quite some time."

That made Quentin smile. He felt honored that Avery felt proud enough to show him off to her parents.

She found her mother and father holding court with

several other prominent socialites. Her parents smiled as she and Quentin approached.

"Thank you for coming, sweetheart." Her mother kissed either cheek and gave her shoulders a gentle squeeze. "I know we haven't been on the best of terms."

"You know I wouldn't let you down," Avery replied.

"Well, I must say," Veronica Roberts stepped back to peruse her daughter's new haircut and sequined black halter dress, "you look smashing. The new haircut suits you and so does the gentleman standing next to you. And you are?"

"Quentin Davis." He extended his hand. "Pleasure to meet you, Mrs. Roberts." Veronica shook his hand while giving him the once-over.

"MOM, I really need to talk to you," Avery said, when the evening was winding down. Avery had tried for as long as she could to keep the news inside, but she'd made the decision to meet her biological mother and now she had to tell her mother. Most of the guests had long since left and her mother was wrapping things up with the caterers and event staff while her father and Quentin sat sharing an after-dinner sherry. Her father was probably in protective mode and giving Quentin the third degree.

"Darling, it's really been a long evening, can't this wait until tomorrow?"

"I wish I could, Mom, but it can't," Avery replied.

"Please can we talk outside on the terrace? There's really no easy way to tell you this," Avery started.

"You've found your biological mother," Veronica stated matter-of-factly.

"I have."

"And what do you want from me?" Veronica asked derisively. "My blessing? Because you're not going to get it, Avery." Avery began to speak, but her mother held up her hand. "I've had a lot of time to think over the last few weeks. Your father and I have discussed this many times and although I've come to understand why you have to do this, I don't think it's a good idea. Baby," her mother stroked her cheek, "I think this will bring you nothing but pain."

"I don't believe that," Avery replied. "Do you ever think it might bring me peace of mind?"

Her mother shrugged. "Perhaps, but I don't believe so. And despite my reservations you're going to go through with it anyway, aren't you? You're going to confront her?"

"Yes, I am, mother," Avery replied, with a firm tone.

"Well, if I can't talk you out of it, then so be it." Her mother turned and walked off the terrace.

"Mom, wait!" Avery shouted, but her mother had already made it back to the dining room. She saw her whisper something in her father's ear. When he turned and glared at Avery, she felt two feet tall. Like she'd been scolded when she was child for misbehaving. Didn't they understand she had to do this? Avery watched Quentin shake her father's hand and her parents leave the ballroom without a backwards glance at her.

ON THE SHORT flight from Manhattan to Buffalo, Avery had a lot of time to imagine the scenario of meeting her biological mother for the first time. They went from highly optimistic to hopelessly negative. Because fact of the matter was, Avery had no idea how Leah Johnson would react to seeing the child she'd given up for adoption standing on her doorstep. So Avery sat in her rent-a-car outside the Johnson's residence, a five-bedroom mansion in an exclusive subdivision in Buffalo. What else could you call an estate spread out over five acres with a swimming pool and pool house?

"I'm scared, Quentin." Avery couldn't resist calling him from her cell phone as she waited outside in her car on the street. She'd been staring at the house for over half an hour. She'd seen Leah's husband and daughter, *her half-sister* leave for school and work respectively and yet she hadn't found the courage to walk up to the front door and face the mother who'd given her up for adoption thirty-three years ago.

"You've driven that long way," Quentin said on the other end. "You can't chicken out now. You can do this, Avery. You're tough as nails. And trust me, I know because that's the woman I met last month who gave me hell when I crashed her art show."

Avery remembered that woman all too well. Who'd

have known how important Quentin would become in her life. "Thank you, Quentin." She appreciated his support.

"Call me later," Quentin said.

"I will," Avery promised and ended the call. Taking a deep breath, Avery exited the car and walked across the street and up the Johnson driveway. She was sure Leah was still there because she hadn't seen her leave.

"Here goes," Avery said and rang the doorbell. It seemed like several long excruciating moments before the door swung open and Avery got her first glimpse of Leah.

Avery stared openmouthed trying to take in all of Leah's features from her smooth café-colored skin to her round face, pert nose and almond shaped brown eyes. With a sophisticated auburn shoulder-length crop, slender jeans, crisp white shirt and pointy toe shoes, Leah Johnson didn't look fifty-four at all. She didn't look like she was a day over forty.

"May I help you?" Leah asked.

"I, uh . . ." Avery found it hard to find the words.

"If you're trying to sell something, I'm really not interested," Leah replied. "I was just on my way out." Leah began to close the door when Avery reached out and grabbed the door.

"I'm not trying to sell you anything," Avery said, finding her voice. "I'm . . . I'm Avery Roberts. And I'm your daughter."

ELEVEN

It was Leah's turn to stare back at her dumbstruck. "Ohmigod!" Leah's hand went up to her mouth.

"I know this must come as a shock," Avery began, "but I only just found out I was adopted last month."

"I guess I always knew this day would come," Leah said, "but once you'd turned eighteen and no one ever came . . ." Her voice trailed off.

"You figured you were in the clear?" Avery inquired. They were definitely not off to a good start.

"Forgive my rudeness," Leah said, not answering her. "Please come in." She swung the door open. Once Avery was inside, she glanced around the impressive two-story foyer which housed a foyer that no doubt led to the bedrooms upstairs.

"Would you care for some coffee?" Leah replied. "There's still some left from breakfast."

Avery nodded and followed Leah past the formal

living and dining room and into the impressive chestnut-inspired kitchen complete with double oven and island. "You have a lovely home," Avery commented, sitting down at the table that overlooked a large pool.

"Thank you," Leah replied, taking a mug out of the cabinet and pouring Avery a cup from the brewer. "Cream? Sugar?" she asked.

"No thanks. I believe this is an occasion for black coffee," Avery responded to Leah's attempt at small talk to avoid the obvious elephant in the room. Avery watched Leah stand awkward by the island unsure of what to do next. "I'm sure you're wondering why I'm here."

"That's pretty obvious," Leah replied, wringing her hands. "You want answers. You want to know why I gave you up."

"Partially," Avery replied. "The other is I just wanted to know who I looked like."

An "o" formed on Avery's lips. Apparently, she hadn't thought that maybe just maybe Avery would like to know where she came from.

Leah shrugged. "Well, now you know."

"Did you ever wonder about me?" Avery blurted out. She had to know if she'd ever crossed Leah's mind in thirty-three years because from her standoffishness, Avery thought not.

Leah paused before answering. "I did, but I knew I gave you to a good family where you would have a mother and a father. And at that time, I had nothing to offer you."

Avery nodded. "I see."

"I suppose now you hate me after seeing all this?" Leah swung her arms around. "You see the life that was denied you."

"Is that honestly why you think I'm here?" Avery queried. "Because I want something from you?"

"I don't know, Avery, why are you here?" Leah asked, folding her arms. "Because I can't go back. I can't change the past. I made a mistake in my youth and I did the best that I could."

"So, I was a mistake?" Avery fought back the tears that threatened to spill out.

"I didn't mean it like that."

"No, then how did you mean it?"

"Avery, listen." Leah came toward the table and pulled out a chair to sit down. "I was twenty years old when I gave you up. I wasn't ready to be a mother. I was still in college and had no means to support myself, let alone you."

"What about my biological father?" Avery replied. Because his name was suspiciously absent from her original birth certificate from New Hampshire.

"He wasn't an option," Leah returned, standing up. She didn't want to go down that road. What was in the past was the past and Leah wanted to keep it that way.

"Why not?" Avery pressed. She'd come here for answers and she was not leaving until she got them.

"Because!" Leah shouted and faced the pool.

"I have right to know," Avery replied, standing up. "You owe me that much."

Apparently that struck a chord, because Leah came

back and sat down at the table. So Avery joined her. "Why don't you just take it from the top and tell me what happened." Avery reached over and patted Leah's hand to reassure her that she could speak. Leah looked up at her as if she was surprised that Avery would offer comfort and empathy. *Had she expected anger?* If so, Leah was out of luck because Avery was fresh out.

"I, uh. . ." Leah stammered and moved her hand out of Avery's grasp. "I met your biological father at a party thrown by one of his cronies. Mind you, I had no place being there as I was under twenty-one, but I wanted to seem mature and sophisticated. So, I passed him, hoping he'd notice me and he did."

"And?"

"He was a few years older than me and therefore extremely appealing to a foolish girl like me." Leah's eyes misted up. "He drove me home after the party and one thing led to another . . ."

"So I was the product of a one-night stand?" Avery finished.

Leah shook her head. "No, it wasn't like that. Richard and I were more than just lovers. We struck up an affair. And I thought we were headed toward marriage until I found out I was pregnant and he was engaged to another woman."

"What happened when you told him you were pregnant?"

"He offered to pay for an abortion. And I told him no way," Leah replied. "Whether you believe this or not, you were the product of love, Avery. Richard felt obligated to marry the woman his father had chosen for him."

Avery was surprised that after all these years Leah could actually defend the man after he'd deceived and used her.

"As much as Richard cared for me, he couldn't go against his father's wishes or he'd be cut off."

Avery was disgusted. "So he chose money over you? Over love?"

"Yes, he did. And I made the decision to have you and give you up," Leah replied. "And I'm sorry Avery, if I had to go back and do it all over again, I'd do nothing differently."

"So you have no regrets about giving me up? None at all?"

"Did you have a good life?" Leah asked.

"Yes."

"Parents that loved and cared for you?"

"Yes."

"Then I did the right thing," Leah replied. "I did what was in your best interests. Not mine."

Avery didn't appreciate Leah's martyr routine because it didn't ring true. "Your interests were not entirely selfless, Leah. You did it for yourself too. Because you didn't want to be tied down to a child and a single parent. You took the easy way out."

"You have no idea what it felt like to be in my shoes," Leah retorted. "You have no idea what it was like to have to give the child you'd carried in your womb for nine months up to complete strangers all with the belief that they would take care of her."

"But you did!" Avery shouted. "You did it with a backward glance. You didn't even hold me after I was born."

Leah was shocked. "How did you know that?"

"Because my father told me you'd refused to see me."

"And I suppose you think I'm heartless?" Leah asked.

"Aren't you?" Avery asked, rising from her seat and coming toward her. "How could you give up your baby girl without even looking at her?" Avery's voice rose with each question. "How could you?"

"Because if I saw you, I'd never be able to give you up!" Leah yelled back at her.

Avery wished she could believe that. "And now?" Avery asked. "I'm here now..."

Leah swirled around to face Avery's tear-stained face. Avery waited for Leah to open up her arms and envelop her, but she didn't instead she shook her head. "I'm sorry. I can't, Avery. I know this must hurt you, but I can't."

It stung Avery to hear those words. "Why not? I'm here now. Why can't you embrace me now?"

"I have a new life now, Avery. A family. A husband. I'm not the same Leah Gordon that I was back then."

"The family you speak of is my family too," Avery responded. "They are my brothers and my sister."

"Who have no idea that you exist," Leah replied. "You see, I never told my husband that I had another child. Do you know what this would do to my marriage? To my children?"

"Your children!" Avery shouted. "I'm your child too. Do you have any idea what you're doing to me?"

"I'm sorry, Avery," Leah cried, "but it can't be avoided. I am so sorry, but I can't acknowledge you. We can't have a relationship."

Avery wiped a tear from her cheek. "Fine. Fine. If that's the way you want it. Fine. But I want to know who my real father is."

"Avery, no!" Leah shook her head.

"Either I leave here with his name," Avery began, "or I will shatter this perfect little family that you've created. I want his name, Leah, and I want it now." Deep down Avery would never tell a soul, but Leah didn't know that. Avery wouldn't want her siblings to feel the kind of pain she was feeling at this very moment. But emotional black-mail was all she had to get the truth out of Leah.

Leah turned her back and considered her options. Her husband would most certainly leave her if he ever found out she'd had another child and had lied to him throughout the course of their marriage. He was a proud man and well-respected in the community. "Alright," Leah said, turning around. "I'll tell you."

Avery folded her arms. "I'm waiting."

"I'll tell you, Avery but you have to know that he's a very successful businessman now and I doubt things will turn out any differently than with me," Leah replied.

"It doesn't matter," Avery replied. "Now that you've shown me what to expect, I won't have any expec-tations."

Leah felt as if a knife had been stuck in her heart, but she had no choice. "His name is Richard King."

"Richard King?" Avery repeated the name. Of all the names she'd expected, it was most certainly not that one. How could her father be the very same man Quentin was shooting an expose on and the one his friends despised? The very same man that could walk away from the mother of his child, an inner voice responded back.

"I'm sure you've heard of him," Leah said. "The King Corporation is well-known throughout Manhattan."

Avery nodded. She was in complete and utter shock. Richard King was her biological father? So, Leah had an affair with a Caucasian man. Well, that explains a lot. She'd always felt she must be mixed, but now she knew.

"I'm sorry, Avery," Leah continued. "I wish we could have a relationship. But given my husband's standing in the community if this came out, it could damage his career."

"And I wouldn't want to do that." Avery replied, rising to her feet. "Thank you for the information." She slung her purse over her shoulder and headed towards the kitchen exit.

"What do you plan to do?" Leah asked.

Avery couldn't believe her nerve and swerved around to glare her biological mother for what would be the only time they'd meet. "That isn't any of your business now, is it?" Avery asked. She gave Leah one final withering look before storming out.

. . .

THE RIDE to the airport and subsequent flight home was a blur for Avery. How could she not be in a fog when Leah chose to abandon her for the second time and her biological father turned out to be a lying, ruthless snake like Richard King? Once she'd landed at the airport and turned her phone back on, Avery noticed that Quentin had called several times, but Avery couldn't talk to him right now.

She was having a hard enough time processing the news, let alone trying to explain it to another person. She was deeply hurt that Leah had turned her back on her. She hadn't expected a miracle or her to throw her arms around her, but she hadn't expected her to not to want to have anything to do with her either. Leah didn't even so much as touch her. Would her presence have truly been that disruptive? Avery would never know because her Leah had an icebox where her heart should be.

"QUENTIN, IS EVERYTHING OKAY?" Dante asked when he kept staring at his cellphone every few minutes.

"I'm sorry, Dante," Quentin replied. "I'm just waiting for a phone call." He'd been waiting for Avery to call him back and tell him how the meeting with her biological mother went, but she hadn't called. He'd left several messages and she still hadn't responded. He was worried.

"From Avery Roberts, I presume?" Dante asked. "For someone who claimed this was only a bet, you sure have spent a lot of time with the lady the last month." Dante wasn't blind. Quentin had fallen for the art buyer but refused to admit to anyone including himself.

"I suppose I have," Quentin replied. "Dante, Avery has surprised me more than any woman ever has. I thought she was cold and haughty, but now that I've gotten to know her, she's the exact opposite. She's really quite warm and sincere and did I mention extremely passionate."

"And we know how important that is to you," Dante replied, smiling. "Seriously though, I'm glad you've found someone to make you happy even if did start with a bet. Did you even tell her about that?"

"No, I haven't. I doubt she'd be too thrilled with me."

"You never know. Maybe she'll take as a compliment that you wanted to get to know her," Dante said, hoping he sounded optimistic.

"I doubt that," Quentin shook his head. "She'd take it as an insult, because initially I did think she was all those things, but I was wrong."

"Then admit that too," Dante suggested. "Honesty is always best."

"Where did honesty get me with Malik?" Quentin replied. Quentin hadn't seen a hair on Malik's head since he'd walked out on him last month. "It got me nowhere," Quentin replied answering his own question.

"You have to end this war with Malik, Quentin."

"Any suggestions on how I do that?"

"Well . . . talking it out might help."

"He doesn't return my calls."

"Then confront him and don't let up until he stops being so stubborn," Dante replied.

"I'll take your advice to heart," Quentin replied, pulling his wallet out and sliding a ten Dante's way for the beer.

"What are you doing?" Dante pushed the money back his way.

"Listen, my friend," Quentin left the money on the table and walked to the door, "you need all the paying customers you can get. Why don't you stop being so stubborn and take the money, ya hear?" Quentin said. He pointed at the money on the bar before leaving.

"I'll do that." Dante smiled and put the money in the cash register.

QUENTIN DECIDED to wait to call Avery again until the evening. He'd thought about it and perhaps she was emotionally drained and needed some time to herself. It's not every day you meet the mother that gave you up for adoption. If so, he would give her a day or so and if she didn't call him, he was going to find her.

Quentin focused his energies during the afternoon on his last shadowing session with Richard King before the Manhattan Chamber of Commerce crowned him Businessman of the Year. Quentin was glad this assignment was nearing its end. Then he could finally repair the damage that had been done to his relationship with Malik. He just hoped it wasn't too late.

"I know you'll be working in an official capacity, Quentin, but will you be bringing a date to the gala?" Richard inquired after his meeting had ended.

"I hadn't really thought about it," Quentin replied. He was there to do a job, not socialize with the opposition. He'd done the honorable thing and abided by the commitment his agent had made for him. He didn't want to spend more time with Richard King, because try as he might he was finding it hard not to like the guy.

"You should bring one," Richard returned. "You can sit at my table with me and my wife Cindy."

"That really isn't necessary."

"I insist," Richard responded. He was not a person to take no for an answer. He was used to getting what he wanted and for some reason this photographer had intrigued him. Because it was clear, he didn't want to be here so why did he stay? Why had he kept this assignment even though it was clear Richard stood for everything he was against? The question had puzzled Richard the last couple of weeks, and he was dying to know the answer. Perhaps, his date might shed some light on the man.

"All right. I'll ask her, and if she doesn't have any plans she'll be there."

"Fair enough. I look forward to meeting the lovely lady." Richard held out his hand to Quentin. For a moment, Quentin thought about not shaking it, but always the professional, he accepted Richard's proffered hand.

"I'll see you Saturday night," Richard replied. He

strutted out of the room with his advisor right behind him like a puppy dog.

Once Richard had left the room, Quentin wasted no time in getting on his cell and calling Avery. His call immediately went to voicemail which meant she had her cellphone turned off. He tried the gallery next, but the intern told him that Avery had called in sick. Quentin knew something was off. Avery had gone a full twenty-four hours without telephoning him and now she hadn't gone to work. And for her to take a day off with the way Hunter had been riding her, Quentin was worried. Had something happened to her in Buffalo? Quentin quickly packed up his belongings and exited the building.

Outside, he hailed a taxi and had it drive him to Avery's apartment. "Put your foot on it," Quentin ordered. He was anxious to find Avery. He shouldn't have waited. He should have listened to his first mind and checked on her yesterday. As soon as the taxi stopped, Quentin paid the fare and hopped out.

He raced past the doorman and took the stairs instead of the elevator. Despite his athletic physique, he arrived out of breath to the tenth floor and banged on Avery's door. "Avery! Avery, are you in there!" Quentin knocked on the door.

Avery was in bed when she heard Quentin banging on the door. She threw off the covers, slipped on her robe and headed to the foyer. "Quentin, go away, please," Avery said through the door. "Please just go away. I just want to be alone."

"Avery, please open up," Quentin pleaded. "I don't know what happened between you and your biological mother. But whatever happened, you can talk to me."

"I can't see you right now, Quentin," Avery replied. "Just go away."

"Avery, let me in or I'm going to break this door down!" Quentin stated firmly.

Avery had no doubt that he would do exactly that if she didn't open the door. "Fine!" Avery yelled, swinging open the door. "Are you happy now?" She turned her back to Quentin and walked back to her bedroom. "I just wanted to be alone. Why couldn't you give me that?"

"Because I was worried about you," Quentin returned and with good reason. Avery was mess. Her hair hung flat and limp at her shoulders, her eyes were red and puffy and she was wearing a pair of pajama bottoms and a stained NYU t-shirt underneath an old robe. "What happened with Leah, Avery?" She didn't answer, she just walked past him to her room and got underneath the covers. Determinedly, he followed behind her and stood in the doorway. "Avery, I asked you a question."

Avery bolted upright. "She rejected me, okay?" she yelled as tears spilled over onto her cheeks. "You were right. She didn't want to have anything to do with me. Don't you want to say you told me so?"

"Avery, I'm so sorry." Quentin rushed over to the bed. He pulled Avery into his arms and smoothed her hair with his hand. "I didn't want to be right. I hoped that she would welcome you with your open arms."

"That didn't happen, Quentin," Avery replied. "I don't know why I expected anything to be different thirty-three years later. I was an inconvenience. She didn't want me then and she didn't want me now."

"What can I do?" Quentin asked, cupping her face in his hand. He wanted to ease her pain, but he didn't know how. "What can I do to make this better?"

"There's nothing you can do," Avery replied, bitterly. "It is what it is. And I just have to accept that." Avery threw herself to the bed and turned away from him.

"Then I'll just stay with you here for the rest of the day and all night if have to," Quentin returned, untying his shoelaces. He took off one shoe and then the other before joining her underneath the covers.

"You don't have to do that."

"I know I don't have to." Quentin snuggled behind her until her bottom was resting firmly against his groin. "But you're stuck with me, so just accept it." He wrapped his arms tightly around her. Quentin wanted her to know that she could count on him.

WHEN AVERY AWOKE the next morning, she found her bed empty. She rubbed her eyes and glanced at the clock. It read ten a.m. Had she really slept that long? And why had Quentin left in the middle of the night? He could have at least told her instead of sneaking out. Avery didn't know why she was upset. Perhaps because he'd come to mean more to her than she cared to admit? Last night, he'd been a rock. He'd let her talk and cry or just remain silent. She'd needed him and he'd been there for her more than any man ever had. That's why it was so upsetting to find him gone in the morning light. "Maybe he's in the kitchen," Avery said aloud and padded to her galley kitchen. When she arrived, she found it too was empty. "Great, thanks a lot, Quentin."

UPTOWN, Quentin stood in front of the Roberts' door and rang the bell. In his dreams, he'd been struck with the best medicine to cure Avery and she opened the door a few minutes later: her mother, Veronica Roberts.

"Hello, Mrs. Roberts," Quentin smiled. An older, more sophisticated version of Avery stared back at him. "I don't know if you remember me from Vegas night. . ."

A light came into Veronica's eyes. "Oh yes, you're the gentleman that accompanied my daughter. How can I help you?"

"Well, it's not me you can help, Mrs. Roberts. Right now, Avery needs you."

"Why? Is something wrong?" Veronica asked. "Did something happen to my daughter?" Worry creased her forehead.

"It's more like who happened to your daughter," Quentin returned.

Veronica knew exactly what he meant. "Let me grab my purse."

They arrived twenty minutes later and Veronica used

her key to let them in. "Avery!" Veronica called out to her daughter.

From her bedroom, Avery heard a voice that sounded like her mother, but she thought she was hearing things until she heard her name again. "Mom!" Avery rose from her bed.

Quentin and her mother were standing in the foyer. When Avery saw her mother, she ran toward her and her mother enveloped her in her arms. "My baby," her mother crooned in her ear.

"Mama," Avery cried, "I'm so sorry. I'm so sorry." Avery hugged her mother tighter. "I should have never done it. You warned me. Please forgive me."

"It's okay, Avery. I'm here now and that's all that matters. And there's no forgiveness needed. I'm your mother and I will always love you."

Quentin felt like king of the world, when Avery looked up at him with tears in her eyes and mouthed the words, "Thank you". Quietly, he stepped back and exited the apartment to give the two women some much-needed bonding time.

TWELVE

"I'm in love with him, Jenna," Avery revealed two days later when she joined her for coffee. Now that she'd faced the past and reconciled with her mother, Avery felt like a giant load had been lifted off her shoulders and she could finally breathe again. Sure, she still hadn't adjusted to the news that Richard King was her father, but that was another story entirely.

What overwhelmed her the most was her growing feelings for Quentin. He'd come through for her in a real way the last few days. He'd bridged the gap between her and her mother and they were on solid ground. No, make that better than they were before she'd found out she was adopted.

"I knew it," Jenna replied. "From the moment you saw him, I felt the sexual tension between the two of you."

Avery shook her head. "I admit, there was that. But it's more than sexual attraction now, Jenna. Quentin's a wonderful man. He's kind and compassionate. And caring. The way he's taken care of me the last week has been nothing short of amazing."

Jenna eyes widened. "That good, huh?"

"Better." Avery grinned from ear-to-ear.

"So, what's next?" Jenna asked excitedly.

"What do you mean?"

"Well, are you two a couple now?"

Avery thought about it for a moment. Jenna asked a good question. Were they a couple? They sure hadn't discussed being in a committed relationship, but that's exactly where they were. At least she was. She wasn't seeing anyone else. And she doubted he had the time to squeeze anyone else in. "Honestly, Jenna, I don't know. We've never actually discussed it."

"Has he admitted he's in love with you?"

Avery shook her head. "No, but I feel it. Why is it always difficult for mean to express how they truly feel?"

"I don't know, girlfriend," Jenna replied. "If I had the answer to that question, I'd be a wise woman. But seriously, you should talk to Quentin and tell him how you feel."

"I'm scared, Jenna. What if he's not ready for a commitment?"

"You'll never know unless you ask him."

"I'll give it some thought," Avery replied. She wasn't sure if she was willing to put her feelings on the line again after what happened with Leah. Maybe it was better to play it safe.

. . .

LATER THAT EVENING, she joined Quentin at the tapas bar. He was finally going to introduce her to his friends. Avery took that as a step in the right direction. Men didn't usually invite you to meet their friends unless they were serious. At least that what she told herself when she walked inside.

She found him congregated at the bar with the attractive woman from the gallery opening and another good-looking brother she hadn't seen before.

"Avery," Quentin rose and came over to greet her, "you look beautiful as always." Quentin loved the strapless mosaic dress with empire waist. "C'mon, I want you to meet my friends." He walked her over to the bar. "Dante, Sage. I'd like you to meet Avery Roberts."

"It's a pleasure to finally meet you," Sage replied, coming forward and shaking Avery's hand. She gave Quentin a knowing wink. So, Q finally had the guts to bring her to meet them. He was definitely in love, thought Sage. But since her dear friend had never been in love before he just didn't know it.

"You too," Avery said. "I've heard a lot about you both," Avery smiled at Sage and Dante. "And Malik," she added.

"Well, uh, perhaps you'll be able to meet him another time," Dante replied.

"I sure hope so," Avery replied. "You guys are the four musketeers, right?" Avery looked up adoringly at Quentin.

And when she did, he noticed something he hadn't dared let himself see before. Was Avery falling for him? Because the way she'd smiled up at him just now certainly indicated those feelings.

"Well, once upon a time we were," Quentin commented sadly.

"And we will be again," Dante replied, "Come join us, Avery. I was just preparing some dishes for everyone to enjoy."

Dante had arranged a corner table for the group and it was decked out with a wide assortment of tapas dishes. Avery's mouth watered as her eyes and nose got a feast for the senses.

Hours whizzed by as they all drank wine and ate the delectable food Dante had prepared, who'd taken the night off and let his sous-chef handle the kitchen.

Avery laughed at their funny anecdotes as they reminisced about their growing pains living at the orphanage. Avery didn't have any stories to add because she was an only child herself. She couldn't help but marvel at how well they all turned out after such a hard childhood. Quentin was a renowned photographer, Sage a lawyer, Dante a chef and restaurateur and even Malik was a community center director. They had thrived despite the obstacles life had thrown at them.

It was a lesson Avery was being tested on herself. Faced with the knowledge that her biological mother didn't want to have anything to do with her was sobering to say the least. In her head, she understood why Leah rejected her. She was from a wealthy family as well and her father certainly didn't need the scandal. Imagine the gossips on the Upper East Side, discussing the fact that she was the illegitimate daughter of Richard King? Her mother would die of embarrassment. Thank God she didn't know. And Avery had no intention of telling her.

"Avery, what do you think?"

"What?" Avery had been daydreaming. "I'm sorry I missed what you said."

"Sage asked if you'd seen the Color Purple on Broadway yet?" Quentin asked.

"I thought we might all get together one night for a night on the town," Sage replied, smiling at Quentin.

"I'd like that," Avery said. She'd never had many close friends outside of Jenna and looked forward to opening her social circle to include Quentin's friends. They were good people and she told him as much later back at his loft while they lounged on his sofa.

"Tonight was really great," Avery commented. "Thank you for inviting me. I really like your friends."

"They're my family," Quentin corrected. "Without them, Avery, I don't know how I would have made it. And they liked you too. You got their seal of approval."

"I'm glad that you had them and you weren't alone," Avery said, stroking his goatee. "I just wish I could have met Malik."

"Another time," Quentin replied, bending down and kissing her neck, "Because right now," he nuzzled her ear with his nose, "I have something else in mind entirely." He reached over behind her and unzipped her dress. It fell in a pool in her lap, exposing her beautiful shaped breast to his riveting male gaze. "Hmmm," Quentin groaned before bending down and feasting on lusciously brown nipple. He teased it until it turned into a rocky pebble.

"Oh yes," Avery whimpered. "More."

Quentin lathed it with his hot, wet tongue. She tasted so good and so sweet.

"WHAT ARE YOU DOING TOMORROW NIGHT?" Quentin asked, turning on his side so he could face her. He'd avoided asking her all week because she had so much on her plate, but he was obligated to attend the New York Chamber of Commerce Businessman of the Year Awards, because he needed to get the final shot of Richard for his photo expose for Entrepreneur.

"We didn't have any plans, did we?" Avery's brow rose.

"No, but I have to go to this stupid awards gala. I don't really want to go, but I have no choice."

"Who's it for?" Avery queried.

Quentin rolled his eyes. "Richard King."

"W –who?"

"Richard King. The guy I'm doing the expose on. The reason I've ruined one of my longest friendships." Quentin's tone was cold and harsh and not lost on Avery. "So, what do you think?"

"Well, when you make it sound so appealing, how can I resist," Avery said. If she went to the Awards dinner with

Quentin, she would finally be able to see Richard King in person rather than just a photo on the internet. After her experience with Leah, she wasn't prepared to go after Richard King with guns blazing and reveal her existence. She'd learned her lesson the first time. This time, she would look before she leaped.

"What time should I be ready?"

"Seven o'clock."

AS SHE STOOD in front of her hall mirror for one final perusal in her asymmetrical one-shoulder long-dress with a side slit, Avery was curious about how Richard would look. Would it be like staring back at an image of herself? Would she look anything like him? From the picture online, she couldn't tell if he had green eyes. She was adding a touch of lip gloss when the doorbell rang. She'd wanted to give Quentin a key but felt that might be giving away too much of her feelings so instead, she'd remained silent.

"You look breathtaking," Quentin said, giving her a whirl. "And might I add sexy as hell." He looked at the slit and the incredible expanse of long leg it gave him. He was going to be rock hard all night just thinking about taking that dress off her slender body. She was rocking that dress!

"You're pretty dapper yourself." Avery enjoyed the view of him in a Joseph Abboud tuxedo with satin lapel. The jacket emphasized his broad shoulders and massive chest. He'd brought his camera with him to take some final pictures of Richard as he accepted his award.

"Are you ready to go? I've hired a driver for tonight."

"You mean we're not going to ride on your Harley?" Avery asked, smiling as she threw her gloss in her beaded clutch purse.

Quentin eyes traveled from her rhinestone-studded sandals to her hair which despite the shorter length she'd managed to pin in a loose chignon with bangs. "Not in that dress, honey."

"I'm glad you noticed," Avery said, grabbing her wrap from the back of her sofa and heading toward the door.

"Oh, I noticed," Quentin said, turning off the lights and closing the door behind him.

The driver drove them to the Ritz Carlton in Battery Park where the Businessman of the Year Award was being held in the ballroom. When they arrived on the second floor, guests had spilled out into the foyer as they waited for the banquet to get underway. As soon as they entered the room, Avery scanned the room looking for Richard King. She hardly noticed the silk wallcovering, chandeliers, gold plated chairs and linen tablecloths.

"There he is," Quentin pointed across the room to Richard who standing with his wife Cindy and several other couples. Avery's eyes flew across the room and immediately landed on Richard. As if he knew someone was staring at him, he looked over and smiled. He motioned for Quentin to join him. "C'mon, I might as well introduce you."

"Wait a sec," Avery said and smoothed her hair and

dress down. Proudly, she took Quentin's arm and walked toward Richard King, her biological father.

"Everyone, this is world-renowned photographer, Quentin Davis," Richard introduced him as they approached. "He's doing a photo spread on me for Entrepreneur."

"Excellent," another man said, patting him on the back. "It's well deserved. You've had a great year, Richard."

"I've heard of you." Richard's wife Cindy came forward and shook his hand. "I'll never forget those pictures you took on 9/11."

"Thank you," Quentin replied.

"I don't believe we've met." Richard came toward Avery. "Quentin, why don't you introduce me to the lovely lady."

"Richard King, meet Avery Roberts." Quentin turned sideways. "Avery's an art buyer for the Henri Lawrence Gallery in Soho."

Avery didn't know how to react when Richard brought her hand to his lips and brushed his mouth across it. "It's a pleasure to meet you Avery."

Avery was at a loss for words when he looked up at her and she found a pair of green eyes staring back at her.

"Avery?" Quentin whispered in her ear.

"Oh, I'm sorry." Avery snapped out of her haze. "It's a pleasure to meet you, Mr. King," Avery said, staring back at him.

Richard seemed taken aback when he looked at her.

"Has anyone ever told you that you have the most striking pair of green eyes?"

"Kind of like yours," Avery added, smiling back at him.

"Are you flirting with my girlfriend?" Quentin asked Richard jokingly. He wasn't so sure he liked the way Avery was staring back at King. Surely, she wasn't entranced by all the trappings of his success. He'd found her to be much more down to earth than that.

Avery turned sideways and smiled at Quentin. Had he just called her his girlfriend? It was funny how one word could make her feel all warm and fuzzy inside despite the fact that she was standing in front of her biological father and he was absolutely clueless.

"Of course not," Richard said, stepping back and grabbing his wife's hand. Even though something about the young woman seemed oddly familiar, he just couldn't put his finger on what it was. "I only have eyes for one woman."

"Oh honey," Cindy King leaned over and kissed him on the cheek and then lightly wiped off the lipstick smudge with her thumb.

Over the course of dinner, Avery caught Richard staring at her several times, but then he'd look away and Avery would wonder if she'd imagined the whole thing. Perhaps she was manifesting her own subconscious desire for Richard to suddenly realize she was his daughter onto him.

When Avery stepped away to powder her nose with his wife, Richard took the opportunity to whisper in

Quentin's ear. "Avery is a lovely young woman, Quentin. How did the two of you meet?

"At the opening for one of her artists," Quentin returned. "Initially, she didn't care for me, but there was no denying there was something between us."

That's when it came to Richard. Avery reminded him of another time long ago, heck, another lifetime when he'd laid eyes on a beautiful woman with café-au-lait skin with whom he'd instantly fell in love with. It was a shame that life happened and he hadn't been able to fulfill his own dreams.

"Sounds like she's stolen your heart," Richard replied.

"She has," Quentin answered honestly.

"Have you told her that?"

"No, I haven't."

"Don't waste too much time, my friend. Sometimes life has a way of sneaking up on you and getting in the way. You'd better grab hold of her and hold on for dear life."

"Sounds like you've lost a woman yourself, Richard."

Richard nodded. "I did. I lost someone very dear because I was stupid and too scared to get out of my own way. Don't let the same thing happen to you." Richard rose from his chair and stepped away to join another group.

When Avery returned and Quentin lightly swept his lips across hers, she asked, "What was that for?"

"Do I need a reason to kiss you?"

"Of course not." Avery leaned over to give him another kiss.

Shortly thereafter, the chairman of the Manhattan

Chamber of Commerce came forward to the podium and announced Richard King as Businessman of the Year. Sitting there and watching him accept the award, Avery realized what a well-respected man Richard was. She doubted he'd appreciate the scandal of an illegitimate bi-racial child coming forward any more than her parents would. Even though she knew she would never say anything, she still wanted to know more about the man. That's why when he invited Quentin and her back to his suite, Avery quickly accepted.

"I don't know." Quentin was tired of the monkey suit and all the polite chitchat. He'd wanted to unwind in bed with Avery.

"C'mon at least join me and my wife in my suite for a night cap," Richard said. 'It's got a great view of the New York Harbor, the Statue of Liberty and Ellis Island."

"Sounds great," Avery said excitedly. "Doesn't it, Quentin?"

He couldn't help but notice the way her eyes lit up when she asked him, so he had no choice but to go along. "All right, but only for one nightcap."

Nearly an hour later, one nightcap had turned into two along with Richard and Avery on the sofa engrossed in a conversation on art.

"You should come to the gallery," Avery said. "I have some great pieces that I'm sure you'll love."

"I'd like that," Richard replied. "I'll have my assistant call you and set up a time on Monday." There was something so warm and engaging about Avery Roberts that he'd seemed powerless to stop himself even though he sensed some hostility coming his way from Quentin. His interest in Avery was not sexual, it was more mercurial.

"Great."

On the other sofa, Quentin was fuming. He'd hoped to have a quick drink and then take Avery back to his place. He'd planned on stripping that dress off her body and ravishing her all night long, but his plans had been averted and he was none too pleased. *What was the fascination with those two?* he wondered. Avery was mesmerized by King and it bothered the hell out of him. "Avery, it's getting kind of late." Quentin stood up and looked at his watch.

"Ohmigod," Avery glanced down at her Cartier watch. "I didn't realize it was so late. I'm sorry to have kept you, Mr. King."

"Please, call me Richard."

Avery grinned. "Richard, it is." Avery rose from the sofa and Richard did the same. He walked them both to the door. "I look forward to introducing you to the gallery." Avery shook Richard's hand.

"As do I." Richard returned the handshake. "Quentin." He nodded to him. "It's been a pleasure working with you. I can't wait to see your expose."

"Richard." Quentin nodded. He breathed a sigh of relief once he and Avery were outside the suite. Once they were at the elevator, Quentin turned to Avery. "What was that all about?"

"What was all about?" Avery asked, feigning ignorance. She knew Quentin wasn't pleased at her attention being elsewhere during the evening, but it couldn't be helped. She'd just met her biological father!

"You and Richard were hemmed in together half the night," Quentin responded.

"Were you jealous?" Avery asked, cozying up to his side. "Because if you are," she kissed his jawline, "I assure you, you have nothing to worry about. Matter of fact, I'll make it up to you." Avery kissed the other side of jaw. "All night long."

Avery was brazen in bed that night as she unleashed her inner sexy and Quentin let her. He enjoyed this unrestrained side of Avery. Not that she hadn't been that way before in bed, she was naturally expressive and passionate, but this time was different. She was the one in charge and he was loving every minute of it.

She stripped him down to his briefs and pushed him back on the king-size bed while she slowly unzipped her dress. He watched the fabric fall in a puddle on the floor leaving her wearing nothing but a skimpy thong.

He sucked in a deep breath when she slowly pulled her thong down leaving nothing on. She was pure temptation. "Oh yeah, baby," Quentin groaned, devouring her with his eyes soaking in all the sweet lines of her slender body and as she came toward him crawling on the bed, Quentin was ready for her. His shaft was straining against the confines of his briefs until she pulled them down and released him.

She leaned over him and reached inside his drawer for

a condom. "Would you like me to do the honors?" she asked.

"Yes," Quentin said never taking his eyes off her.

"But first, I have something else in store for you," Avery dipped her head and took him all the way inside. *Oh God, was the last thought* Quentin remembered as Avery teased him with her gifted mouth. When he felt himself about to lose control, he gently pushed her back onto the bed. He couldn't wait; he desperately needed to be inside of her.

He grabbed either side of her hips and pressed forward. When the tip of his erection found its mark, he slowly eased deep inside. Her felt her muscles clench and pulse around him, causing him to thrust forward. Avery encouraged him by titling her hips upward allowing him to thrust again and again. Over and over. His orgasm came long and strong. He felt Avery's body jerk as she climaxed Stronger than any he'd ever had in his life. And that's when he knew – there were no ifs ands or buts, she was made for him. Avery had touched a part of him that he'd thought was closed off forever. He was in love with Avery Roberts.

THIRTEEN

Richard King's assistant telephoned Avery on Monday to schedule an appointment for him to come to the gallery to peruse some of their artwork for his home collection. Despite her desire to remain aloof to his existence, she couldn't help but be excited at the prospect of Richard coming to her domain. She'd even taken special care when dressing for the day.

Thankfully, she'd stashed a new outfit at Quentin's loft which consisted of some tan wide leg pants which she teamed with a silk cami and a tapered leopard-print jacket. And with her stylish hairdo, Avery looked every bit the polished art buyer that she was. Surprisingly, Richard arrived later in the morning alone. Avery and Hunter were discussing their next exhibition when he walked in.

"Excuse me, Hunter," Avery said and walked toward Richard. "My appointment is here." She didn't notice the jealousy that came across Hunter's face that the wealthy businessman in the Armani suit was her client.

"Avery." Richard clasped both her hands and kissed both her cheeks. He stepped back to take a look at her. "You are looking well, my dear."

Avery smiled. "Thank you, Richard. So, are you ready to see my gallery?" she said, tucking her arm in his.

"Absolutely." Richard smiled back at her. "Lead the way."

Richard nodded to Hunter as Avery led him through several of the gallery's popular artists and her new find, Gabriel Thomas. Avery could feel Hunter's eyes on the back of her head as she and Richard laughed and talked about the awards banquet.

"You know, Avery, I must say, I can't recall a time when someone has charmed me more. Quite frankly, you've put a spell on me and I'd buy anything you want me to."

"In that case," Avery said, moving Richard to some of the more exclusive artwork, "let me show you . . ." But she didn't get a chance to finish because Hunter interrupted them.

"Hello." Hunter extended his hand to Richard. "I'm Hunter Garrett, *Director* of the Henri Lawrence Gallery."

Avery noted the way he said 'director' as if she were nothing more than a peon. "Hunter, I have this. Thank you."

"I'm sure do, but did you—"

"Mr. Garrett, was it," Richard said, staring Hunter

straight in the eye. "I expressly came here to see Ms. Roberts. She's a skilled curator, is she not?" Avery appreciated Richard sticking up for her.

"Well . . . yes, but I have—

Richard turned stone cold. He wasn't used to being interrupted, especially not by the likes of him. "If I will be buying an artwork for the King Corporation or my home collection, it will be from Avery."

Take that, Hunter, thought Avery. Realizing he'd overstepped, Hunter nodded and scurried off upstairs to his office, blessedly leaving Avery and Richard in peace.

"Thank you for that, Richard," Avery said. "He's been riding me for months now. You really put him in his place."

"I'm glad. I didn't like the way he was treating you. Matter of fact, why don't you come to the King Corporation and I'll put you in charge of my collection."

Avery's eyes widened in amazement. "Are you serious?" She was stunned. "That's a really generous offer."

"Yes, I'm serious. You're a smart, talented woman and someone who would be a great asset," Richard said folding his arms. "Think about it, okay?"

"I will." Avery couldn't believe how kind he was being. He hardly knew her.

"Good. In the meantime, I'll take those two there." He pointed to two paintings that combined would put her way over the top in commissions this month. "And I'll take the last two pieces of your new artist's work."

"You've no idea what this means to me," Avery said.

Richard winked at her. "I have some idea. Now, listen,

I have to get going. I have a lunch meeting. I'll have my assistant contact you for payment and delivery." Richard headed toward the door.

"Sounds fantastic!" Avery beamed. Once he'd gone, Avery let out a whoop. "Yes!" She brought her hands down to her side. She was on her way to her office to write up the order when she found Hunter at the top of the stairs watching her.

"Looks like you made quite the sale," Hunter commented.

"Yes, I did," Avery replied, climbing the stairs.

"How did you manage to land a big fish like Richard King? We are a small gallery, after all. First, we have Quentin Davis interested in exhibiting and now King. What gives?"

"Are you wondering what you don't have, Hunter?" Avery asked, sarcastically.

"I know, what it is," Hunter said, folding his arms across his chest. "Clout. You grew up in the Upper East Side, therefore you have connections, unlike me."

"What I have, Hunter," Avery said, standing up her tiptoes and whispering in his ear "is talent and Richard recognized it."

With that comment, she strutted past him and into her office.

QUENTIN WAS in his darkroom processing images from the last couple of months. He'd decided that black and white would pack the most punch and allow him the most creativity, when he came across the photos he'd taken at the community center. There were some great pictures of the young dance troupe practicing and even better ones of the young man he'd hoped to mentor taking a jump shot.

Right then, Quentin realized what he had to do. Quentin decided to go to the center and confront Malik head on. He was not one to run from his problems. He'd let this feud go on long enough between him and Malik and it was time he ended it.

For the rest of the afternoon, he put the film on Richard through the chemical process of developer, a stop bath and fixer. He was hanging them to dry when he heard a knock on the door. It was Avery.

"I see the red light is on," Avery said from the other side of the door. She'd noted the red button was flashing above the darkroom. "Can I come in?" She'd let herself in with the key Quentin had given her. Clearly, there was no one else or he would have been afraid to give her a key for fear of someone finding out. They were definitely making progress.

"Yes, you can come in," Quentin said. "I'm just about finished."

"It's kind of cozy in here," Avery said, commenting on the amber-colored lighting. "Actually, I would say it was romantic." She came forward and wrapped her arms around Quentin's middle.

Quentin felt the heat of her on his back. Felt the warmth of her breath against his neck. And it caused his temperature to rise. He immediately turned around and planted a sizzling kiss on her lips. "Hmm, I like the way you think." Quentin said, circling his arms around her waist and gently pulled her towards him. He captured her mouth in his. Quentin slipped his tongue inside and began a mating ritual that was as old as time itself.

It was a soul-stirring kiss that left Avery feeling light-headed and a molten sensation quickly spread throughout her body. She clutched his neck and pressed her breasts against his rock-hard chest. She felt electrified, tantalized and extremely sexual, but they were in his work room with a lot of chemicals.

She pulled several pictures of the pictures from the community center out of the clips. "These are really great, Quentin. Who should really see these is Malik," Avery commented. "You never set out to hurt him, Quentin. Don't you think it's time you hang up your macho pride and make this right? Go talk to him." Avery knew how difficult it was for Quentin to remain at odds with Malik.

"It's too late," Quentin replied. "It's been months. He's not going to listen."

"You mean he's as bull-headed and stubborn as you?" Avery inquired. "Then you both have that in common. You both have drawn a line in the sand and neither one of you refuses to give in inch. Is this how you honor your long-time friendship?"

Quentin smiled. Avery had a point. Perhaps it was time he hung his pride on the shelf and tried to end this feud between him and Malik. "All right, all right, I'll make an effort. Are you happy, now?"

Avery smiled. "Yes, I am."

"Good," Quentin said, pulling her back into his arms so they could finish where they left off.

"Don't you want to ask me how my day went?" Avery asked.

"Sure."

"Work was fantastic!"

"That good, huh?" Quentin couldn't remember Avery describing any time spent in Hunter's company as fantastic. "How so?"

"Richard King came in and not only brought several paintings, but he put Hunter Garret in his place," Avery said moving out of his arms. "You should have seen it." Avery's hands flew up in the air. "Hunter tried to steal my sale and Richard told him in no uncertain times that he would buy from me or not at all."

"Wow," Quentin, folded his arms. "Sounds like Richard really came through for you."

"In a big way," Avery smiled. "He even offered me a job as a corporate buyer at the King Corporation."

"He did!"

"Yes, it was pretty amazing offer."

"And what did you respond?"

"I told him I'd think about it."

"Avery, if you don't mind my asking," Quentin replied, "what is the fascination with King?"

"Oh, I don't know. I've certainly met powerful men

before, but there's something about him." Avery tried to dodge the question. "Are you jealous?"

"Maybe a little," Quentin answered honestly. "The way you look at him . . ."

"Doesn't even come close." Avery pulled him towards the exit. Minutes later, they were falling back onto his bed as she said. "Why don't I show you who's really on my mind."

THE NEXT DAY QUENTIN TOOK ,mDante and Avery's advice and went to the community center to make peace with Malik. He'd allowed this nonsense to go on much too long. He was determined to end this once and for all.

"Malik Williams, please," Quentin said to the hard-nosed receptionist.

"And your name, sir?"

"You don't remember me?" Quentin asked. "I'm a friend of Malik's. I was here photographing the center."

"No, I'm sorry, I don't remember you," the older woman shook her head. "What's your name?"

Man, the woman didn't give an inch. She was just like that old battle ax, Vivienne Falconer, who'd been recep-tionist since his adolescence. "Quentin Davis."

She buzzed Malik and from her facial expression, it was clear Malik said he didn't want to see him. "I'm sorry, he's in a meeting right now."

"He's not busy, he's just being a stubborn mule," Quentin said, pulling open the front door.

"You can't come in, sir." The woman rose from her desk and tried blocking Quentin's path, which was really quite useless considering he was over six feet to her five-feet four. "I told you Malik was in a meeting."

"And I told you, ma'am," Quentin's voice rose as he tried to remain respectful "that I need to talk to Malik."

"Q, stop bullying my staff," Malik replied from behind her.

"We need to talk, Malik."

"Now is not a good time," Malik said, turning his back and walking towards his office.

"It hasn't been the right time in two months," Quentin casually side-stepped the elderly and less quick Vivienne and followed Malik into his office. "Enough is enough, Malik. I've given you two months, which was more than enough time and space to get over this. When are you going to let this go?"

"I'm not," Malik answered.

"So, you intend on keeping up this charade forever?" Quentin asked, "You may be used to not having me around, but it must have been awfully lonely the last two months without Dante and Sage around."

Malik threw back his dreads. "I've been just fine," Malik lied. Quentin was dead right. He hadn't realized just how much his family meant to him until they were no longer in his life. Over the past few months, there had been many times he'd wanted to reach out to them, but how could he when he'd made an utter fool of himself? He'd blown the whole affair way out of proportion, of course. He knew Quentin hadn't intentionally set out to hurt him, but it still stung nonetheless.

"Sure, you have," Quentin said. "Malik, you're like a brother to me and I'm sorry if I disappointed you, but I had to do the right thing."

"You mean what was best for your career?"

"Can you blame me?" Quentin finally asked the question that had been logged in his throat for a long time. "You know as well as well as I do what it's like to do without. Can you blame me for not wanting to trash my career?"

Malik took a deep breath. "No, of course not. I was just really counting on your help, Quentin."

"I know Malik and I feel terrible. What can I do?"

"Well," Malik thought about it, "can't you show both sides of the story? You know, showcase Richard King, but also show the consequences of one of his big development deals: showcase the community center."

Quentin thought about Malik's suggestion. He'd taken some great photographs of the center. What better way to highlight their struggle than to show the services they offered the community? Quentin smiled. "I think that's a great idea," Quentin replied, "I'm not sure how my agent or Entrepreneur's editor is going to feel about it. But I can at least present the photos and give them the option."

"You would do that?" Malik asked.

"Of course I would," Quentin returned. "I'll do

anything I can to bridge this gap, so we can be friends again."

"Awww, Q." Malik couldn't resist Quentin's sensitive side and came forward to give him a long overdue hug. "Are you going soft on me, man?"

"Not a chance." Quentin patted his back and stepped away.

"I DON'T LIKE IT, QUENTIN," Jason told him when he stopped by his office the following day. Quentin had brought with him the shots of Richard in his office, at one of his construction sites in a hard hat and one of him at the awards dinner all juxtaposed against a photo of him pointing to the community center and the subsequent shots of the clinic, the dancers and the boys playing basketball.

"I don't agree," Quentin replied. "Those pictures are pretty powerful."

"Exactly my point," Jason replied haughtily. He hated to disagree with one of his best clients, but he had a duty to do what was in his best interest, whether Quentin liked it or not. "They're negatively depicting King and that's not what you were hired to do."

"I'm delivering what they hired me for," Quentin returned. "There are always two sides to every story and I'm showing the other."

"Entrepreneur wants to highlight Richard King

achievements, not show what a ruthless businessman he is. I think it's a bad idea."

"Well, I'm not asking your approval," Quentin responded. "Out of professional courtesy, I came to tell you what I was planning to do. I plan on delivering both sets of pictures."

"Despite my *professional* advice."

Quentin shrugged. He was not backing down. This was important to his friendship with Malik and heck, that center was important to him. Sometimes in life you had to make a stand, and this was one of those such moments for him.

"This is career suicide, Quentin. You're at the top of your game. Why would you purposely sabotage yourself? Once word gets around that you're a prima donna and can't take direction, you'll be finished. Is that what you want? To end up back on the street hustling? Because that's exactly where I found you." Jason's words were harsh, but they needed to be said. When Quentin didn't respond, Jason said. "Fine, have it your way, but don't say I didn't warn you."

Jason's ominous warnings stayed with Quentin throughout the course of the evening. Even when he and Avery had stepped out for dinner, he couldn't shake the feeling.

"Is everything all right?" Avery asked. "You haven't been yourself tonight." She'd watched him push the food back and forth on his plate, hardly eating a bite. And Quentin loved to eat, though you could hardly tell because he kept himself in shape at the gym or with the weight machines he kept in his loft. His body was lithe and trim and gave her immense pleasure, she smiled at the though.

"No, I had a disagreement with my agent today,"

"Oh?" Avery became uneasy and fidgeted in her seat. She sure hoped Quentin wasn't jumping ship and flying off to God knows where. Isn't that what photojournalists did?

"Yeah, I told him that I had a different angle on the photo expose on Richard King."

Avery perked up. Now she was really curious. He was talking about her biological father after all, which she hadn't yet told him. "How different?" she asked, taking a sip of her wine.

"Well, I've decided to send the magazine the photos of Richard, but also some photos on the center. I'm hoping they'll see the story potential on this. You know, here this rich and powerful man is destroying a community all in the name of greed."

"Quentin, how can you say that? I thought you liked Richard."

"Just because I think that overall he's an alright guy doesn't mean that I'm going to agree with everything he does. Especially when it comes to tearing down a place that's near and dear to my heart," Quentin responded. "And why is it you're defending the man? Since when did you become his biggest champion?"

"Since he came to the gallery and bought several paintings," Avery replied.

"Oh please, that was nothing but a drop in the bucket to him." Quentin didn't believe King's motives were altogether altruistic. He was probably just trying to impress Avery.

"Thanks a lot," Avery replied. He made it sound like her knowledge of great artwork had nothing to do with it.

She rose from her chair so quickly it nearly fell back. Quentin caught it before the chair tumbled to the floor.

"I'm going to go and powder my nose." Avery stormed to the women's room to calm her frayed nerves. Immediately, her hand came to her mouth. Why had she reacted like that? Because Quentin wanted to prosecute Richard in the media. Not that she could blame him. He had no idea who he was or what he meant to her because she hadn't told him.

She'd kept the secret to herself not so much as to protect King but to protect herself and her parents. She and her mother were finally back on track and this would put a wrench in that. Not to mention the embarrassing scandal. But what should she do now? Even though she owed him nothing, she couldn't knowingly let Quentin publish those photos of Richard. Could she?

When she returned to the table, Quentin came around to help her with her chair. "Listen," he began, "I'm sorry if what I said offended you. I in no way wanted to imply that Richard wouldn't recognize what a great artistic eye you have. Because you are extremely talented, Avery. And I don't even know if I've ever told you that before, but you are. I think you're amazing. No, make that incredible."

"Thank you," Avery replied. That was exactly what she needed to her. "I think you're pretty incredible too."

"Then let's get out of here." Quentin threw a hundred dollar bill down to take care of the tab.

Once back at Avery's apartment, he undressed and peeled off each layer of her clothing like an onion, leaving her without a stitch on. Quentin wanted to savor every inch of her the way she was meant to be savored. His blood ran hot and heavy through his veins.

He slipped inside the bed and gathered her in his arms. He drew her mouth to his. "Are you ready to be naughty?"

Her answer was a scoot to the middle of the bed giving him plenty of access to have his way with her.

He lazily circled over each of her nipple with his hot urgent. Then his lips began moving lower to her belly-button where his tongue played havoc. Then he was moving farther south, lowering his head to tease her core causing her body soared at the intimate contact. His tongue embarked on a sensual exploration which sent white hot darts of desire flickering through her.

"Oh yes," her groans were deep and guttural as Quentin took her on a sensual journey.

He quickly put on protection putting the condoms he'd purchased to good use. He sucked in a sharp intake of breath as he entered her. He felt her tight haven stretch to accommodate him. When she wrapped her legs around him he thrust harder and faster going deeper until he brought them to brink of an orgasm. A cry of pleasure escaped her lips and shudder tore right them and he collapsed on top of her.

"Quentin, I really need to talk you," Avery finally said.

It was time she told Quentin the truth about her connection to Richard King.

"Hmmm, what about?" Quentin nuzzled her neck with the tip of his nose.

"About Richard King."

"Not again," Quentin sighed. "What is it about this man, Avery, that has you so enraptured?"

"Quentin, there's a lot you don't know," Avery begun.

"So, why don't you fill me in?"

"Well," Avery rose to the seated position. "Quentin, you see . . ."

"Whatever it is, just spit it out."

"When I was Buffalo, Leah told me the identity of my birth father,"

"She did?" Quentin was shocked. Before he could ask another question, he realized that Avery had kept this information to herself for months. "Why didn't you tell me you got back?"

"Because I was grappling with her rejection."

"And since then?" Quentin wasn't letting her off the hook that easily. The more he thought about it, the angrier he got, she'd had plenty of time to tell him the truth.

"And since then, I decided I didn't want to know. That it didn't make a difference.

"And now it suddenly does? Why?"

"Because my biological father is Richard King."

"Richard King!"

"You heard right," Avery replied to Quentin's shocked expression.

"Wow!" Quentin fell back against the pillows. He sure hadn't seen that one coming.

Avery turned to him. "Imagine how I felt when I learned the news. It was pretty amazing that my boyfriend just so happens to be doing an expose on Richard King."

Quentin mulled the information over in his head. "Well, this certainly explains your fascination with the man."

"I have no intention of telling Richard the truth," Avery replied.

"Why not?"

"Because he never wanted me to begin with because he was already engaged to Cindy even though he was having an affair with Leah. He asked Leah to get rid of me," Avery said, "but she couldn't."

"So she gave you up instead."

"And after her reaction, I can't take another rejection, Quentin. My heart can't handle it."

"So, why bring him up now?" Quentin didn't understand. "If you have no intention of telling him, why tell me?" She could have kept the secret forever and he would have been none the wiser.

"Well. . ." Avery didn't know how to begin. Although Richard King was no father to her and had no idea who she was, she still didn't want to see him hurt.

Then it hit Quentin. Avery wanted him to nix his idea

of running the photos of community center. Quentin fixed his dark eyes on her. "You don't want me to send those photos in of the community center, do you?"

Avery was afraid to look at him because she'd felt a distinct chill enter the air.

"I asked you a question," Quentin said, his fury starting to rise. How could she ask him to go against Malik again? When she knew how desperately he wanted to repair their relationship? And for Richard King of all people? He wasn't in need of her protection; he was a big boy and could clearly take care of himself. The community center could not.

"Yes," Avery finally nodded. "I don't want you to send those pictures to Entrepreneur."

"How could you ask me to do that?" Quentin stared back at her. He couldn't believe this was the same woman he'd just made exquisite love to. Who knew him so intimately, but yet in the same breath, could ask him to betray his best friend.

"Because he's my father!" Avery said vehemently.

"Clayton Roberts is your father," Quentin returned, threw back the covers and started picked up the clothes he'd discarded earlier. "As you stated yourself, Richard King has no idea who you are." Quentin began dressing.

"What are you doing?" Avery asked.

"I need to get out of here," Quentin said, "before we say something we're both going to regret."

"Quentin, please don't leave like this," Avery said, reaching over to the bottom of the bed and pulling on her robe. She put in one arm and then other and turned to face him. "Can't we talk about this?"

"What is there to talk about, Avery?" Quentin asked.

"I know I am asking a lot," Avery began.

"Avery, you're asking more than a lot," Quentin replied. "You're asking me to choose. To choose between you and my family."

"Aren't I worth it?" Avery asked. "Or have I been nothing more than a bedwarmer for you the last few months, Quentin?"

"That's a low blow, Avery."

"Is it?" she asked. "Not once have you ever mentioned where we're headed. Not once have you ever said you cared for me."

"Are you kidding me," Quentin said. "I've shown you, Avery. In every way I know how. I've shown you."

"But you've never said the words, Quentin."

"So, is this a test, Avery?" Quentin asked. "Are you testing me to see how deep my feelings for you run?"

"What if I am?" Avery said defiantly, folding her arms across her chest.

"Then I guess I just failed," Quentin said, storming out of her bedroom.

Once Quentin had gone, Avery collapsed onto the bed. What had she done?

FOURTEEN

Avery was wreck. She hadn't heard from Quentin. She'd left several voicemails, text messages, heck she'd resorted to email and still nothing. She had made a terrible mistake backing Quentin into a corner and asking him to choose between her and his family, but what choice did she have? She was trying to protect Richard.

Thanks to him, she'd had several more clients or referrals of late at the gallery, and even Hunter had to comment on how well she was doing.

"I hate to admit it," Hunter said during a discussion on an upcoming exhibit. "But despite your head being elsewhere, sales at the gallery sure haven't suffered."

"If that's your back handed way of complimenting me," Avery said, "then thank you. And since the gallery is doing so well, I'd like to ask for an increase in my commission."

"Well. . . I don't know about all that."

Avery was not backing down. She'd waited a long time

for this moment and she was in a position to push the envelope. "I've brought in most of the clientele to this place, but if you'd like me to take that someplace else . . ." Avery shrugged

Hunter thought about it for a moment. He couldn't afford to lose someone with Avery's talent and connections. Mr. Lawrence had expressed just the other day how happy he was with the gallery's sales.

"I'll present this to Mr. Lawrence," Hunter replied, "but I can't guarantee you anything."

Avery smiled. She had it in the bag. "Of course, but I'm sure you'll do your best to persuade him. Now if you'll excuse me, I have a lunch appointment." Avery rose and headed for the door. And for once, Hunter didn't ask where she was going or who with. She had finally proved to him and Mr. Lawrence how valuable she really was and it felt marvelous!

"IS EVERYTHING OKAY, Q?" Dante asked, walking toward him. Quentin had come into the bar over an hour ago asked for a bucket of beer and had sat in one of the booths looking forlorn as he chugged each one.

"Far from it," Quentin answered, placing an empty bottle on the table.

"Don't tell me," Dante said. "I'd know that look anywhere. You're having woman troubles."

"You're right on the money, Dante," Quentin asked.

"What happened? If you don't mind my asking?"

"It's complicated," Quentin replied, "but suffice it say, Avery asked me to make a choice. And either way I lose."

"Sounds ominous."

"It is."

"Look on the bright side, you made up with Malik and now everything can go back to normal?"

"Can it?"

"Of course, it can. He's stopping by for dinner with Sage," Dante glanced down at his watch, "in an hour or so."

Great, thought Quentin. That's exactly what he needed. To be faced with the flip side of the coin. If he didn't send those pictures that would for certain be the end of his friendship with Malik and he doubted Dante and Sage would be too happy with him either. But on the other hand, despite how angry he was with her for asking him to choose, he didn't want to lose Avery either. She had become as important to him as breathing itself. But if he went forward with those pictures, their relationship was over.

Malik and Sage showed up an hour later and it was as if the last few months hadn't happened. The four of them laughed and talked and teased each other just as they'd always done except this time, it meant more to Quentin than he'd ever realized because what if this was the last time they were together as a family.

"We missed you, you little pigheaded mullet," Sage said, pulling Malik into a warm, bear hug.

"I missed you too, kiddo." Malik kissed Sage on the

forehead. "And I'm sorry that I didn't return your calls. I know you were trying to help."

"Yeah, well if I wasn't so busy trying to make partner and working crazy hours, I would have really given you a piece of mind."

Malik had no doubt she would. Sage was a real spitfire. "Then I'm glad I escaped your wrath."

"Just barely," Sage said smiling. She glanced back and forth between the three men. She was so happy they were all back together again. She'd hated the distance between them. Sure, she had other friends, but these guys were like home. "Group hug, group hug."

"Aww, Sage." The men bemoaned her attempt at lovey-dovey.

"C'mon, give me some love," she said, opening her arms. Reluctantly, Dante, Malik and Quentin joined her in a group hug. "Now doesn't that feel better?" she said when they separated.

"Great!" Dante said. "Who wants a drink?"

"Me?" Quentin said.

"I think you've had enough," Dante commented, popping open a beer and sliding one Malik's way. Quentin had finished the entire bucket of beer.

While he and Malik chatted, Sage walked up to Quentin. "Okay, what gives?" she asked. "You've been moping since we got here. What's going on?"

"Nothing."

"Bull. Try again."

Quentin laughed. Trust Sage not to take no for an answer. "Avery and I had a disagreement."

"Is that all?" Sage chuckled. "Those happen in relationships. Oh wait, you usually don't stick around for that."

"Thanks, Sage. I really appreciate your help," Quentin replied, walking away.

"Hey," Sage stopped him. "You know I was just kidding. I'm glad to see that you're in a relationship. It was high time you stopped kissing and running."

"Yeah, well I don't how to deal with all of this, Sage. I thought I knew. I thought that if you loved someone, the rest would be easy."

Sage's eyes grew wide. "What did you just say?"

Quentin's brow furrowed. "What do you mean?"

"Did you just say you loved Avery?"

"Of course not," Quentin lied and shook his head. "I don't believe in that love thing."

"I know what I heard," Sage said, pointing her finger at him. "Don't be afraid to admit that you love her, Quentin. I'm sure Avery wants to hear you say it. You guys have been joined at the hip the last few months."

"If this is what love feels like," Quentin said, "then I don't want it. I can do without it." He didn't like not feeling like he was in control of his emotions. It scared him.

"The heart feels what it feels," Sage said, grabbing Quentin by the arms and pulling him back towards the bar. "You can't control it."

Those words stuck with Quentin for the duration of the evening. And somewhere between dessert and the cab ride home, Quentin realized he didn't want to live his life without Avery in it. "You can drop me off at Seventy-Ninth and Central Park West," Quentin asked the cabbie.

"Sure thing."

When he rang Avery's doorbell it was nearly ten o'clock. He hoped he wasn't waking her. He was unprepared for her to open the door and throw her arms around his neck. "I'm so happy to see you," Avery said, furiously kissing him on the neck.

Quentin pulled back. "I'm happy to see you too."

"Quentin . . ." Avery began, but he silenced her by putting his forefinger on her lips. "I'll do it," Quentin said. "I won't send in the pictures."

AS SHE SAT down at her desk, the next day, Avery replayed the previous night's events over and over in her head. Had Quentin really come over to her apartment and told her he wouldn't send in those photos? Quentin said he would tell Malik this evening after work. Why postpone the inevitable? Had he really chosen her over his friendship with Malik? It should make her happy, so why did she feel like she had a frog logged in her throat and she couldn't breathe.

"Hunter, what can I do for you?" Avery asked when she found him standing in her doorway.

"Good news!" Hunter replied. "Mr. Lawrence has approved your requested commission increase."

"That's great!" Avery said, feigning a smile.

"Don't sound so excited," Hunter replied. "I had to campaign for you."

Avery doubted Hunter had to do much campaigning her work spoke for itself, but if that's what he needed to feel better, she'd go along with it. "And I appreciate it," Avery replied. "I just have a lot on my mind."

"All right, well I'll leave you to it."

"Thank you," Avery said. After he'd left, Avery decided she needed a pick-me-up and what better way than lunch with Jenna. She quickly dialed Jenna's office and found that she was free.

A few hours later, they were seated at a cafe having salads. "It's good to see you," Jenna said, kissing Avery's cheek. "And the hairdo is still holding up." Jenna touched Avery's sophisticated razor-cut hairdo. She'd been back to Dominic for a touch-up to maintain the look.

"Thanks," Avery said.

"What's wrong?" Jenna asked. "Last we spoke you were in love and on cloud nine."

"I know, I know. And now I've gone and ruined it."

"What did you do?"

"I put him an untenable situation and asked him to choose between helping me and helping his friends. Who are like family to him."

"That doesn't sound too good," Jenna replied. "I don't think that was a wise move, Avery."

"No kidding!"

"Is there any other way to avoid this?"

Avery had been thinking about that all morning. If she

told Richard the truth, perhaps he would reconsider? If he understood how important this was to her, could he find some sort of compromise? "Possibly." Or perhaps, he would take one look at her at think it was a joke and be more determined than ever to build his development. It was a gamble.

"You have to try. If you love him as much as you say, then you can't ask him to do this — even for you."

As soon as the words were out of Jenna's mouth, Avery knew she was right. She'd thought of nothing else all morning. She supposed that's why she'd called her, for confirmation of what she needed to do. It was just last night she'd been so overwhelmed by the depth of Quentin's feelings towards her, she hadn't thought about what this was costing him.

"I know you're right. I'm just not looking forward to what I have to do."

"Well, whatever you need. I'm here for you."

"Thanks, Jenna. I might be taking you up on it later tonight," Avery replied.

Once she returned to her office, she immediately dialed Richard King's phone number. His assistant told her that he was unavailable until after 5pm. "That's perfect," Avery said, hanging up the phone. Now, she just had to reach Quentin before he told Malik. The problem was when she called his cell, it went directly to voicemail. *Where was he?* He couldn't have just slipped off the face of the planet. She just prayed she would reach Quentin before he went to Dante's this evening.

. . .

"SO, you've decided to heed my advice?" Jason asked Quentin when he delivered the photos of Richard King for Entrepreneur as promised later that afternoon.

"Yes, I have," Quentin replied, "but not for the reasons you think."

"So, the plot thickens." Jason regarded Quentin quizzically. He was surprised by Quentin's change of heart; his client was as stubborn as a mule. Jason was sure he was going to shoot himself in the foot. "So what changed your mind?"

"I'd rather not say, just suffice it to know that those photos are exactly what the magazine is looking for to promote King as a successful entrepreneur and businessman."

"All right," Jason said. "Keep your secret. I'm just happy to see that you aren't sabotaging the career you've worked so hard to achieve. Well, I guess our business is concluded for now. I'll touch base with you next week on that Warner Books deal."

"Thanks," Quentin said, rising from his chair and heading toward the door.

"Wait a sec," Jason said, "What about the photos of the center?"

"What difference does it make?" Quentin asked. "They'll never see the light of day, right?" He strode out the door without a backwards glance. Now he had the unenviable task of facing his best friend for the second time and telling him he was reneging on his promise. He felt like such a heel.

He pulled out his cellphone to check his messages and noticed he had four missed calls. All from Avery. He ignored them. He wasn't ready to talk to her right now. Afterward, he would, because she would be all he had left.

THE KING CORPORATION offices were very plush and swanky, thought Avery as she sat down in the waiting area his receptionist had ushered her into. Although she was leaving for the day, she had assured Avery everything was fine and that Richard would be out of his meeting momentarily.

"Avery," Richard came toward her and kissed her cheek. "I was so surprised, pleasantly so, when my receptionist said you requested a meeting with me today."

"Yes, well. . ." Avery was extremely nervous. "It was a matter of extreme urgency and delicacy."

"Well, come into my office," Richard said, opening his arm so she could proceed. "Let's see how I can help."

Once he'd shut the door behind him, Avery stood not sure of how to begin.

"Please have a seat." Richard gestured to the sofa across from his desk.

"Thank you," Avery said and took a seat. She smoothed down her skirt as she prepared to reveal her identity.

"And you asked her to have an abortion," Avery finished.

"But she adamantly refused. She said we conceived you in love, so she couldn't have that procedure. But if she believed that, how could she give you up? Didn't she know I would have supported you both?"

"I guess you'd have to ask her that question yourself," Avery replied. Though she doubted Leah could give him very many answers. She sure hadn't given Avery much. "I never had any intention of telling you the truth, but I need you to do something for me."

"And what might that be?"

"I need you to back off this development deal you have in Harlem that would demolish the community center."

"What?" Richard was confused. "I don't understand, what does this have to do with you."

"Quentin and his friends grew up in that center. His friend Malik Williams runs it and he's done a great job. You can't destroy what he's built."

"And if I don't agree?" Richard asked. "You're going to go public with this information, aren't you?" Was his daughter really prepared to blackmail him? If so, she really did have some of his genes running through her veins.

"No, I'm not," Avery replied. "I'm asking you to do the right thing. The community needs that center. It supplies free healthcare, after-school care and many youth activities."

"I have a lot riding on this deal, Avery."

"I realize that, but I'm asking you to do this for me,"

Avery pleaded. "This really means a lot to me and to the man I love."

"The man you love?" Richard asked. "I admit Quentin Davis is a decent fellow, and I thought very highly of the young man, but you're in love with him?"

"Yes, I am. And that center means everything to him after growing up as an orphan. Without it, he would have never survived Richard." She grasped his arm. "I am begging you, pleading with you, to please reconsider. For me." She added.

Richard didn't know what to say. He was standing in front of his and Leah's daughter. A daughter he never thought he'd have. He and Cindy had never been blessed with any children. After many miscarriages, they'd finally given up on having a child of their own. And Cindy had steadfastly refused adoption, so they'd lived a solitary life just the two of them. And now his daughter, his flesh and blood, was standing in front of him asking him for his help. How could he possibly turn her down?

"All right, Avery," Richard said. "I'll do it."

"Thank you." Avery reached over and hugged Richard.

He didn't realize he'd been holding his breath until she let go.

"You have no idea what this means to me."

"I've some idea," Richard said, "or you would never have come forward. So what now?"

"What do you mean?"

"Can we have some type of relationship?"

Avery was surprised. She'd thought he'd want to sweep

this under the rug. Keep her existence a secret. "Do you want one?"

"If you'll have me?" Richard replied.

"I'd like that," Avery said and then glanced down at her watch. "But I really have to be going." She had to catch Quentin before he said something he couldn't take back. "Thank you, Richard." She rushed out of the room and left him staring after her.

"WHAT'S THE BIG NEWS?" Sage asked as Quentin came rushing inside Dante's later that evening.

"Yeah," Malik concurred. "I love you guys and all, but two nights together? What going on man?"

"I have to talk to you about something and I know it's going to make you all unhappy so thought I'd better get all done at the same time," Quentin said.

"This doesn't sound good at all," Dante commented.

"Does this have anything to do with some photos that you were going to send in?"

"It does," Quentin stated.

"So once again you're selling me out," Malik stated. "Once again, the center loses out. I just don't understand it, Quentin. I thought I knew you but apparently I was wrong."

"Quentin," Sage grasped Quentin and forced him to face her. "you wouldn't do this again. You wouldn't hurt Malik without cause, so why are you now?"

"I can't tell you," Quentin said.

"Oh, no you don't," Malik said. "You can't back down like some coward. Tell us what the big darn secret is that's causing you to go back on your word again."

"I can't say. All I can tell you is this has to do with Avery."

"What does she have to do with why you can't help Malik?" Dante asked.

"I can't break Avery's confidence," Quentin said. He hated that he was between a rock and hard place.

"Avery, Avery, Avery!" Malik yelled. "You know Quentin, *Avery* was supposed to be a bet, a bet which you've seemed to have forgotten. You were supposed to wow her with the Quentin Davis charm, get her into bed and move on. And now you're putting her over me, when did that suddenly change?"

"Malik, I—" Quentin never got to finish, because Sage halted him with her arm and nodded towards the doorway where Avery stood open-mouthed.

"Avery . . ." Quentin came toward her, but Avery put up a hand to halt him.

"Don't!" Avery replied. "I just came to tell you that Richard is not going forward with his development deal."

"What do you mean?" Malik inquired.

"He is backing off. There will be no condos or multimedia complexes going up."

"You're kidding!" Sage said. "How did you manage that?"

"He did it for me," Avery replied. "His daughter." And with that comment, she ran out the door.

Dante didn't understand. "Did she just say his daughter?"

"She sure did," Sage replied.

"But I thought she was adopted?" Dante returned.

"She was," Quentin replied and took off after her.

"I guess that explains why she wouldn't want a negative story on her father in press," Sage said to Malik and Dante.

"And why Quentin refused to have those photos published."

"Because he's in love with her," Malik finished. "And now I just ruined it."

"It's not your fault," Sage replied. "I just hope Quentin can fix this," she said, looking toward the door.

FIFTEEN

Quentin ran down the street and caught up to Avery just as she was hailing a cab. "Avery, wait!" Quentin shouted. In seconds, he bridged the gap between them. "Avery, please stop."

"Why should I?" Avery whirled around and faced him. Her eyes blazed with fury and her face was flushed with rage. It was almost enough to stop Quentin cold, but he persevered. "Clearly, I mean absolutely nothing to you."

The hurt he saw lying in those green depths, tore right through him. "That's not true." Quentin shook his head.

"Isn't it?" Avery asked bitterly. She was furious at him, "I was nothing more than a bet to you, Quentin Davis. You used me for your and your friend's amusement. You guys must really have gotten a kick out of this."

Quentin hung his head. "No, we didn't. And I suppose initially it might have started that way."

"You suppose? Oh, give me a break!"

"But things changed, Avery. The more I got to know you, the more I liked you. You weren't some stuck-up rich girl, you were warm and funny and beautiful and amazing."

"And a sucker," Avery added just a cab pulled up to the curb. "They say one is born every day. And I guess today is my lucky day. Here I was thinking we had something special here. I was way off the mark." Avery opened the taxi door.

Quentin halted her entrance. "Avery, you weren't off the mark," Quentin said. "We do have something. Please give me a chance to make this up to you. To make things right."

"You can't, Quentin. You and I are through. History. Kaput." Avery slid inside the taxi and slammed the door. She rolled down the window and threw out the door. "Lose my number."

Quentin watched the taxi and the only woman he'd ever loved drive away and into the night.

He returned to Dante's and found the crew assembled at the bar. "From your bereft expression, I take it things didn't go well?" Sage asked. Quentin's face was down-turned and he looked in anguish.

"No, they did not."

"Just give her time," Sage said. "She's upset, hurt and probably embarrassed."

"She thinks I don't care about her," Quentin replied. "Why didn't I tell her when I had the chance? All of this could have been avoided."

"Hindsight is twenty-twenty," Malik said.

"I thought you were angry with me." Quentin glanced sideways at him.

"I was, but when it all comes down to it, you're my brother, Q. And the last few months without all of you have been hell. So there I said it. I missed you lugs."

Quentin smiled. At least something good had come out of this. They'd all realized just how important they were in each other's lives. "And we missed you, didn't we?" Quentin looked over Sage and Dante.

"Yes," they said in unison.

"So, is the family drama finally over?" Sage asked, "Because I for one have had my fill of it."

"You and me both," Dante replied. He was tired of being the man in the middle.

"Now, if I only I could get Avery back," Quentin said wistfully.

"You can and you will," Sage said fervently. "I have never known you to give up on something without fight and Avery will be no different. Go find that woman and make her yours."

"MOM, thank you so much for the use of the house in the Hamptons," Avery said the following morning when she stopped at her parents' home before getting on the road. When she called her mother last night, she'd been more than willing to part with these keys.

"It's no problem, sweetheart," Veronica Roberts

replied. "But can't you at least tell me what or who has upset you."

"I don't really want to talk about it, Mother," Avery replied. "All I want to do is get away for a while. You know, get some distance. And I hope some perspective."

"The Hamptons is always a pleasant retreat," Veronica replied. There's nothing more beautiful than walking along the shore collecting seashells or hearing the waves crash outside your window." It would be exactly what Avery needed. "Here are the keys." Veronica pulled a set out of her drawer.

"Thank you."

"How long will you be staying?"

"Oh, about a week or so." Hopefully, after she'd cried her eyes out, she could return to work and get back to the level-headed person she used to be. She didn't even recognize the spontaneous creature she'd become with Quentin.

"Stay as long as you need," her mother said.

"I will, Mom."

QUENTIN HAD TRIED to reach Avery several times over the last couple of days. He'd thought she was avoiding him until he'd finally broken down and called the gallery. That's when Hunter had informed him that Avery had taken a vacation. Where? He didn't know. Her mother was he only person he could think of who would know where she was. So he showed up on her doorstep midweek.

"Quentin, I'm surprised to see you," Veronica said when she opened the door.

"I'm sorry to stop by uninvited, Mrs. Roberts," Quentin apologized.

"You are always welcome," Veronica replied and walked toward the living room. She thought very highly of him. "Please have a seat."

"Oh, I won't be staying long," Quentin said from the doorway.

"All right, well what can I do for you?"

"I'm sure you've heard that Avery and I had a huge row."

Veronica chuckled. "Actually, no. Avery was very close-mouthed on this one. So you two had a fight? That would explain her need for distance and perspective as she called it."

"I made a huge mistake, Mrs. Roberts, and I fear Avery won't forgive me."

"Oh pooh." Veronica threw her hand down. "Quentin, if she can forgive me, she most certainly can forgive you for whatever you've done. Just so long as you weren't unfaithful?" she asked questioningly.

"I was not unfaithful. But I was certainly less than forthcoming. And I want— No, I need to make this right, Mrs. Roberts. I love Avery."

"Of course you do." Veronica smiled. "I knew it the moment you came to get me after her biological mother rejected her. You knew exactly what to do to console her. You knew she needed me. You bridged the gap between me and my daughter and you have no idea how grateful I am for that, Quentin."

"It was my pleasure." Veronica rose and walked over to her desk. "That's why I'm going to help you." She wrote down the directions to their beach house in the Hamptons.

"It's directions to our beach house in the Hamptons."

"Why?"

"It's where you will find my daughter and I hope you'll bring her back to her senses. Because if she lets a fella like you slip through her fingers, it would be a great loss indeed."

"Thank you, Mrs. Roberts." Quentin bent down and brushed his lips quickly across her cheek.

"Oh!" Veronica smiled and touched her cheek. Quentin's eyes were sparking with devilment. "You flirt! You had better get out of here!"

"I will, and when I come back, I'll have Avery with me," Quentin promised.

AS QUENTIN TOOK the two-hour ride to the East Hampton, he recited over and over in his head the speech he wanted to give. He just hoped Avery would let him get it all out. He didn't blame her for being angry with him. She had every right to be. But he had changed from the cynical, commitment-shy man he was when he'd met her. In his previous relationship incarnations, he'd always been quick to leave and on to the next assignment. He'd never had the time for romantic entanglements, but

Avery had been different. With her, he opened up more than he had with any other woman. He'd told her what it was like growing up as orphan. Sure, he'd known love from his grandmother, but when she'd passed she'd taken the love too. He hadn't felt it since, at least not until Avery.

When Avery opened the door, she looked as beautiful as ever with her hair in a ponytail and bare feet.

"What are you doing here, Quentin?" Avery said folding her arms across her chest.

"I came to make things right."

"And how did you find me?" Avery asked even though she knew the answer to the question.

"A little birdie told me."

Her mother. Once again, she had a hard time minding her own business. "Well, she shouldn't have because I don't want to see you. Matter of fact, I want to have nothing to do with you ever again in life." Avery tried to slam the door in his face, but he managed to keep it open by prying his foot in the door.

"Ouch, that's harsh," Quentin said. "A lifetime is a long time. You sure you don't mean for a few weeks, perhaps a month."

"Don't joke with me, Quentin. I am not in the mood. Why don't I say the foreseeable future? Would that suffice?" When he wouldn't move, she swept past and went toward the stairs to the beach below.

"Quite frankly, no it wouldn't." Quentin followed her down the stairs. He didn't care that sand was getting in his shoes. He had come to win Avery back and he wasn't leaving until he did.

"Stay away, Quentin," Avery replied. "Can't you see that I just want to be alone?"

When he didn't answer, she took off running down the shore. He caught up with her and grabbed her by the shoulders and his dark eyes bore into hers. "I am so sorry, okay? I'm so sorry. I should have told you sooner, I was just afraid of losing you."

"Sorry doesn't cut it, Quentin." Avery wrenched herself out of his grasp. "You hurt me. After I gave myself to you so completely."

"I made a mistake. Can't you forgive me? Like you've forgiven your parents? Adoptive and biological? I know you have it within you. You have the capacity because you have a huge heart."

"A heart you broke. And now you're here to pick up the pieces? As if that were possible."

"It is if you allow it to be. If you give me another chance. Avery, I love you."

"Love? You don't know the meaning of the word," Avery said. "You're just saying it now to save face. So your friends will still think you're a great *playa*."

Avery, c'mon think about it," Quentin replied. "If what you say is true then why would I have been ready to trash my relationship with Malik if I didn't love you? I know you put yourself out on a limb for me by telling Richard, but I was willing to do the same for you. I was in essence ending a twenty-year friendship with the only family I've ever had. For you." Quentin tilted her chin and forced her to look up at him. "For you, Avery. Because I love you."

"No, no, no." Avery shook her head and wrenched her arms out of his grasp. "You can't love me. Because I'm unlovable."

"Why would you say that?"

"My own mother didn't want me, why would I think you would? Mr. Smooth Operator. You're used to cutting and running. Why would I think you're in it for the long haul?"

"Because until you I had never found a woman worth throwing in the towel for until now. When I met you, I changed. Can't you see the difference? I feel it. After the childhood I endured, I didn't even think it was possible to fall in love with anyone, but I did. I fell in love with you, Avery. Please."

"My head is telling me to run in the other direction and not look back."

"And your heart?" Quentin asked, stroking your cheek. "What does it say?"

"It says to throw my arms around you and kiss you," Avery said.

"Then do it," Quentin encouraged. "Do it."

Avery couldn't resist him any longer. She had to do what her heart craved. "I love you, Quentin Davis!" Avery shouted and threw her arms around his neck. And when he wrapped his arms around her, lifting her off her feet, Avery knew she'd made the right decision.

"And I love you, Avery Roberts."

Much later, after they'd frolicked on the beach, splashing water on each other, they returned to her parents' home where they began making love. They slowly and languorously undressed leaving their clothes were strewn across the beach house floor, a trail leading to the master bedroom were a testament of their passion. His kisses were tender. His touch sweet. Tears of happiness gleamed in her eyes as Quentin's hands explored every inch of her feminine form, worshipping her.

"Thank you," Quentin said later.

"For what?"

"For giving me and us another chance," Quentin replied. "And for helping me escape the demons of the past. For showing me what true love is."

"You've done the same for me," Avery said stroking his chest. "I've made peace with the fact that I'm adopted and that I won't have a relationship with Leah. And that I could have one with Richard if I so desire. But if I don't, I have two wonderful parents who love me dearly and I'm lucky to have them."

"We've both come a long way in a short time," Quentin said. "After that gallery opening who would have ever thought we'd end up like this?"

"Oh, I had some idea," Avery smiled.

"You did not!"

"Well maybe not in love, but from the moment I met you, I knew I wanted you."

"And you can have all of me," Quentin replied. "Any time you want."

. . .

THE FOLLOWING WEEKEND, Avery and Quentin joined the gang at Dante's for Sage's birthday party. At first, Quentin wasn't sure about coming given the fact that his friends had been in on the bet. He didn't want Avery to think any less of them, but she'd assured him that all was forgiven and it was water under the bridge. She was real trouper and walked in with a smile.

"I am so glad that you forgave him for that bet," Sage said, rushing toward Avery and giving her hug. "It was a stupid bet and we should never had placed it. And I'm truly sorry for my part in it."

Avery interrupted her. "Let's leave that in the past, okay? And start fresh," Avery said.

"You're very gracious. Thank you, Avery. And thank you for coming to my party." Sage couldn't believe she was thirty-years old!

While Avery and Sage chatted, Quentin joined Malik and Dante at the bar.

"I didn't think you had it in you, my man," Dante said, coming forward and shaking Quentin's hand, "but you've found a great catch." He'd never seen Quentin look so happy. From the huge grin on his face, the man was walking on cloud nine.

"I have," Quentin said, glancing at Avery. "And I don't intend on ever letting her go."

"Don't you sound all possessive," Sage replied as she and Avery came toward the men.

"Yeah, I'm a real He-Man." Quentin pounded his chest.

Avery was surprised when Malik of all people said, "Welcome to the family, Avery," and gave her a warm hug. She hadn't seen that one coming. She'd thought he blamed her for some of the trouble within their tight family unit. Apparently, she was wrong, but then again that wouldn't be the first time. She'd misjudged Quentin when she'd first met him.

"Thank you, Malik," Avery said, when he released her. "We appreciate your support, don't we, Quentin?"

When Avery looked up at him with those big green eyes and he saw the love that shone in them, he was overwhelmed. He now had everything he could ever want: a great career, great friends and even better woman.

"Quentin?" Sage said, "Now that you're part of the family, you must call him Q."

"Oh? Well then, I love you, Q, with all my heart and soul." Avery stood on her tiptoes to give him a kiss.

Quentin returned the kiss. "And I love you, Avery Roberts."

BOOKS BY YAHRAH ST. JOHN

The Orphan Series

Playing for Keeps

This Time for Real

If You So Desire

Two to Tango

Adam's Cosmetics

Need You Now

Lost Without You

Formula for Passion

Chicago Nights Duet

One Magic Moment

Dare to Love

Dirty Laundry Series

Dirty Laundry

Can't Get Enough

Hart Series

Entangled Hearts

Entangled Hearts 2

Untamed Hearts

Restless Hearts

Unchained Hearts

Chasing Hearts Pub Date

Captivated Hearts

Mitchell Brother Series

Claimed by the Hero

Seducing the Seal

Guarding His Princess

Stand Alone Novels

Never Say Never

Risky Business of Love

ABOUT THE AUTHOR

Yahrah St. John is not just an author; she's a symbol of ambition and resilience. A Chicago native, now Orlando-based, she's an award-winning romance writer of fifty published books with a career spanning 20 years. Her books, filled with tensionand sensuality and drawn from a well of personal strength, have earned her accolades and a loyal readership. When not writing, Yahrah is succeeding in her other roles as a pioneering property manager while traveling the world and pursuing her latest passion, travel vlogging. Visit www.yahrahstjohn.com to explore more of her world and her work.